STRANGE SENSATIONS

Finding herself suddenly in his arms, Julia felt a flash of panic. Every innate instinct told her to withdraw, to take care. But a wave of heat fogged her senses as she reminded herself of her desire for revenge. Relaxing, she did not resist the strength of his arms encircling her body.

His face was close to hers, and she no longer felt that she could pull her gaze from his. The strong outline of his jaw and the faint glitter of his gaze seemed to mesmerize her. Welcoming this strange—yet extremely pleasurable—sensation, she slowly moved her hands up his chest, until her arms were around his neck.

His arms tightened and she began to breathe fitfully. Feeling herself shiver in his embrace, she knew he was about to kiss her. As she waited, the warmth in the depths of her stomach spread through her limbs. This was nothing like that brief moment on Bolton Street. This was nothing like anything she had ever experienced.

Praise for
A Spinster's Luck

"Talented newcomer Rhonda Woodward penned an enjoyable tale with a mix of mischief and matrimony."
—*Romantic Times*

The Wagered Heart

Rhonda Woodward

A SIGNET BOOK

SIGNET
Published by New American Library, a division of
Penguin Group (USA) Inc., 375 Hudson Street,
New York, New York 10014, U.S.A.
Penguin Books Ltd, 80 Strand,
London WC2R 0RL, England
Penguin Books Australia Ltd, 250 Camberwell Road,
Camberwell, Victoria 3124, Australia
Penguin Books Canada Ltd, 10 Alcorn Avenue,
Toronto, Ontario, Canada M4V 3B2
Penguin Books (N.Z.) Ltd, Cnr Rosedale and Airborne Roads,
Albany, Auckland 1310, New Zealand

Penguin Books Ltd, Registered Offices:
80 Strand, London WC2R 0RL, England

Published by Signet, an imprint of New American Library,
a division of Penguin Group (USA) Inc.

First Printing, December 2003
10 9 8 7 6 5 4 3 2 1

To Mom and Dad
for everything

And to Susannah Carleton
for her wise words, late-night calls,
and warm friendship

Prologue

1815

*O*n the corner of a very fashionable street in London stood five of the highest flying Corinthians the *ton* could boast. To a man, their attention was fixed on a simply dressed, yet exceedingly beautiful, young lady standing on the sidewalk across the street. They watched her with the same intensity she was giving a coach and four lumbering by.

"Damn, Kel, you cannot mean to fulfill the bet with that chit? It is only three of the clock! What if you see a prettier wench at four?" questioned a dashing buck in the steadiest of voices. The others knew this very precise enunciation meant that their friend was quite foxed.

"Dash it, Alton, put a shtopper in it! If Kelbourne shez sheesh the prettyisht gel he has sheen today, then let be. It is between Kel and Dame Fortune anyway," stated the fair-haired Viscount Mattonly, who was not as adroit at hiding his condition as the previous speaker.

The other blades murmured in agreement and vigorously encouraged the tall gentleman standing in their midst to go to it and fulfill his vow.

His Grace, the Duke of Kelbourne, known to his intimates as Kel, ignored his bickering friends, and continued to study the young lady.

A cool sun shone down upon her as she gazed at her surroundings with large, curious gray eyes.

With a decisive movement, he doffed his beaver hat and strode across the street. Dodging stylish high-perch phaetons and closed carriages, he moved quickly lest his quarry disappear.

Miss Julia Allard was enjoying her first visit to London with the real but detached interest of a tourist. As she looked around, she thought again that her childhood home of Chippenham had not prepared her for the cosmopolitan splendor of London.

Presently, she was supposed to be helping her cousin Caroline and Aunt Hyacinth choose bonnet trimmings, but the view from the milliner's shopwindow had proved too much of an enticement. Julia found the bustle exhilarating after living so quietly in the country. At first, the noise, the closeness of the buildings, even the gas lampposts had seemed almost foreign to her.

But now, standing on the sidewalk, she observed all the beautifully dressed people enjoying the fine spring day with pleasure evident on her features. The fascinating scene before her was so captivating, she took no notice of the attention she herself was receiving.

A shiny black coach with a groom riding postilion rolled by. Julia wished Caro had come out; her cousin could identify the owners of the conveyances with only a glance at the heraldic device painted on the doors.

Sighing with satisfaction, Julia reluctantly turned to reenter the shop. She stopped short as a very tall gentleman stepped directly into her path.

Pausing for a moment, she looked up in surprise, before taking a step to the side to pass him.

He stepped to the side also.

Beneath her bonnet, one finely arched brow rose over stormy gray eyes. Julia surveyed the man who was obviously blocking her progress on purpose.

Though he was dressed in perfectly tailored clothing of exquisite fabric, she noted that there was nothing of the fop about him. His deep blue coat fit his broad shoulders as if painted on, and his doeskin breeches and polished Hessian boots accented his powerfully muscled legs.

Her critical gaze traveled up again. He was not classically handsome, but his angled features combined to form a compelling and attractive face. His dark brown hair was styled a little shorter than what was currently fashionable among the beau monde. A straight, rather long nose and bluntly square chin gave him a rakish, formidable air.

A frisson of something that was not quite fear, not quite anger, raced up Julia's spine as she lifted her chin to address the stranger.

"Kindly move, sir. As you can see, you are blocking my path." Her tone was firm, despite her nervousness.

His only response was a slight smile. His assessing gaze continued to sweep her features.

For his part, Kel was greatly pleased to see, upon closer inspection, that her charms exceeded his expectations. It also pleased him that she was so tall— the top of her head came to his chin. A profusion of thick, pale golden ringlets framed a classically sculpted face beneath an attractive bonnet. Her complexion was flawless, smooth ivory tinted with a drop of honey.

He saw large gray eyes, slightly tilted up at the

corners and fringed with thick brown lashes. They were staring angrily back at him.

His gaze settled on her mouth—the goal of his vow. It was full, yet finely defined, competing with her eyes as her loveliest feature.

Once more, he swept her figure with experienced regard. She was slim, but with an understated voluptuousness that would cause men to stare.

Disturbed by this unwanted attention, Julia once more tried to pass him.

Again, he blocked her way.

Panic touched her and she looked around in desperation, noticing that passersby were beginning to stop and stare.

Her uncle had warned her of the debauchery that the beauty of London often hid. Though surely, ladies were not customarily accosted the moment they stepped from a milliner's shop, she thought as her heart began to hammer rapidly.

She took another quick sidestep, and he moved with her. Julia's temper flared. It was time to put a stop to this nonsense.

"Why won't you move?" she demanded.

The man said nothing, only stood there gazing at her with a slightly crooked, raffish smile.

The Duke of Kelbourne was not as disguised as his friends were. He had only imbibed enough spirits at his club earlier that day to destroy his gentlemanly inhibitions, and heighten his already overactive sense of daring.

Nevertheless, the lovely lady's anger was lost upon his dulled senses as he inclined his head in a slight bow.

"I cannot leave you, fair maiden, because of a vow I have made."

"A vow?" This was passing strange. Julia suddenly wondered if this man had escaped his keeper.

"Yes, a vow," he said, and Julia could not help noting how deep and well-modulated his voice was.

"A vow I made last eve to Dame Fortune. I must salute with a kiss the prettiest lady I see today." Turning to the four men who had followed him across the street, he continued, "And this is not only the prettiest lady I have seen today, but the most lovely I have seen in many a Season."

Julia had listened as far as "salute with a kiss" when she decided to turn the other way and quit this ridiculous scene.

She took two full steps before his strong hand caught her arm and pulled her around against his solid body.

"You are mad!" she cried, staring up at him with alarmed gray eyes, shocked as she had never been in the whole of her life.

"Oh no, fair maid, you cannot leave me yet. A gentleman must never break a vow."

Frantic, she struggled, pushing against his chest. She heard one of the other men chortle and say, "I believe Kelbourne is confusing the word *vow* with *wager*."

To Julia's growing horror, a crowd was beginning to gather on the busy street. Besides the men who seemed to be with her assailant, there was a smartly dressed young couple, a few people who appeared to be servants carrying large boxes, and a landau carrying two ladies had just pulled up.

Redoubling her efforts to get away, Julia demanded in a breathless voice to be released.

She also tried to kick his shins, but her skirts and his well-muscled arms clasped around her proved too great a hindrance.

With ease of strength, he dipped her to the side, offsetting her balance so that she had to abandon her struggle.

Julia squeezed her eyes shut, held her body rigid with her hands curled into fists at her sides. His head descended toward hers.

As his lips touched hers she tried to struggle again, but her efforts were fruitless. His arms felt like bands of steel around her straining body. The part of her brain that could think past her mortification wished fervently that she were strong enough to break her attacker's arms.

With his lips on her tightly compressed mouth, Kelbourne was beginning to wonder why the young beauty he held was behaving like a broomstick.

His fogged brain told him something was not right. No woman had ever been anything but eager to be in his arms. In fact, if he could be forgiven for being so immodest, he was usually the pursued, instead of the pursuer.

With masculine determination, he marshaled his considerable personal forces against her defenses.

Julia immediately felt the change in his demeanor.

Suddenly, the kiss became infinitely gentle, the hand on the back of her neck caressed instead of held.

Julia was a mass of jumbled emotions. Rage, fear, humiliation, and something she could not identify, swirled through her senses as she remained rigid in his embrace.

The Duke of Kelbourne raised his head slightly to look at the beauty in his arms. The rage blazing in her gray eyes startled him.

After a sleepless night of revelry and lingering ine-briation, he could only wonder at her fury. He hazily considered the possibility that he had trod upon her toes. Confused, he set her upright and released her.

Shaking with outrage and humiliation, Julia rasped in a voice only those closest could hear, "If I were a man, I'd knock you flat."

She then drew her arm back and slapped him so hard across his face, her palm stung with the force of the blow.

Turning, she cut through the gawking little crowd with a breathless "excuse me" and marched back into the milliner's shop, where Aunt Hyacinth and Caroline were still discussing ribbons.

Chapter One

1816

"**M**r. Fredericks, I insist that you give me back my hand," Julia said, trying to tug her hand free from his determined grasp.

"But Miss Allard, I do not believe you understand the advantages of marrying me." Mr. Fredericks' tone was earnest as he tightened his grip on her fingers.

Julia tugged again, bracing her slippered foot against the base of a nearby stone bench for leverage. Looking up at the house, she prayed that Uncle John or Aunt Beryl would happen by the window, see her struggling with their neighbor, and come out and rescue her from this ridiculous scene.

"Mr. Fredericks, you may see some advantage to marrying you, but I certainly do not. Now, let go before you embarrass yourself further."

The avid expression on his face turned to shocked hurt at the harshness of her words. Julia felt an instant stab of guilt upon seeing the mounting redness in his cheeks as he reluctantly released her hand.

Well, dash it. What do you expect me to do? she

thought defensively as she took a step back from him on the lawn.

She put a hand to her pale golden hair for a moment, and took a deep breath to regain her composure.

"I am sorry to be so blunt, but you have left me little choice," she said, softening her tone.

This was not the first time she had declined Mr. Fredericks' offer of marriage. But never had he been so persistent. It was her suspicion that when he came upon her sitting alone in the garden, he had renewed his courage to propose to her despite her previous refusals.

Allen Fredericks stood in front of Julia, shifting from one foot to the other. The hurt on his florid face rapidly changed to anger.

"What is it, Miss Allard? Do you think you are too good for me because some distant relative of yours is a baron? What does that matter when everyone in Chippenham knows that you were sent home from London last year before the Season began? Such a mystery," he said, sneering.

Julia made no attempt to interrupt him. Inwardly, she marveled that a man, regarded by all in the village as a fine gentleman, could show such ugliness at being thwarted in his desire.

He continued in the same deriding tone. "Some say that you played fast and loose until you were caught. Well, you are no better than you should be, and you aren't likely to find a better man than I willing to take you."

Julia did not attempt to hide her disgust as she looked him square in his white-lashed blue eyes.

"Mr. Fredericks! If you put such store into misinformed and malicious gossip, I wonder at your wanting to marry me. You should consider yourself fortunate that such a *fallen woman* has declined your

offer. I ask you to leave my uncle's property at once."
Her icy tone matched the anger in her gray eyes.

Hesitating, Mr. Fredericks sputtered a bit before
picking up his hat from the bench. He smoothed back
a few thin strands of hair and looked at her, red-
faced and confused.

"Well, I would not go so far as to say that anyone
thinks you are a fallen woman, Miss Allard. It is just
that there has never been an explanation for your
sudden return from London," he muttered, in a weak
attempt to explain his insulting comments.

Julia sighed, looked up to the patch of blue sky
showing through the canopy of trees, and prayed for
patience. That was one of the downfalls of living in
a small village—everyone felt they had a right to
know everyone else's business. Especially tabbies like
the Widow March, who Julia knew had spread most
of the gossip about her curtailed visit to London
last spring.

"Please, Mr. Fredericks, I have no intention of discussing this with you any longer. As you can see, I
was in the middle of reading some letters, and I
would like to continue."

Jamming his hat on his head, Mr. Fredericks had
the grace to look a little ashamed.

"I shall not bother you further, Miss Allard. I bid
you a good day."

Julia stood by the stone bench and watched him
leave the garden through the little iron gate. She sincerely hoped that he would plague her no more.

Sitting down again on the bench, she picked up
the letters she had set aside at Mr. Fredericks' unexpected arrival. Clutching them in her lap to the point
of crumpling them, she thought again of how much
she loathed the Duke of Kelbourne.

Once more, a current trouble could directly be connected to that dastard, she thought with renewed

anger. In fact, every single unpleasant thing that had occurred in the last year could be traced back to that horrible incident on Bolton Street in London.

The fragrant, shaded green beauty of Aunt Beryl's garden faded as Julia's bitter thoughts returned to that time, almost one year ago.

She had been beyond excited when she had received the invitation from Aunt Hyacinth and Uncle Edmund to come to London and make her come-out with Caro.

Such fuss! Such bustle! While Uncle John had stood by, shaking his head, Julia and Aunt Beryl had rushed around preparing for a London Season.

Though the Allards were a fine old family, it was Aunt Hyacinth, formerly a Stanhope, who had connections to the *haute ton*. Even Uncle John had conceded that his younger brother would be able to provide Julia a better entrée into Society.

The only thing that dampened her fervor was that Uncle John and Aunt Beryl would not be coming to London with her. Since the death of her father some ten years earlier, and since she had little memory of her pale, consumptive mother, Uncle John and Aunt Beryl were as dear to her as her parents.

"Won't you change your mind, Uncle John? Or at least come to London a little later in the Season? I shall miss you both terribly," she recalled pleading with him the night before she was to leave for Town.

"And we shall miss you, m'dear. But Edmund and Hyacinth have cultivated London Society all these years, while I am just an old soldier, content to stay in my childhood home with your Aunt Beryl," he had soothingly explained.

So off she had gone with her maid and a groom, full of excited anticipation over the journey, for, except the occasional visits to Bath and Bradford-on-

Avon, she had not been far from home the whole of her life.

Uncle Edmund had taken a beautiful house in Mayfair for his family. Caro had squealed her delight when Julia had arrived. Soon they both had been in transports of excitement over their impending curtsy to the Prince Regent.

London had been a delight to Julia. The museums and the bookstores! She had found something to please her senses around almost every corner.

And then that horrible day!

She could still feel the shock of his insult after these many months.

She recalled that after she had slapped his face and reentered the shop, Aunt Hyacinth and Caro had instantly noticed her pale cheeks and shaking fingers.

"Julia! Are you ill?" Then Caro had called to her mother from the other side of the shop, concern obvious in her blue eyes. "Mama, something is terribly amiss with Julia."

The three women had immediately returned to the house in Mayfair. Aunt Hyacinth had rung for tea, while Julia had struggled to tell them what had transpired.

Caro had sat staring at Julia, her eyes wide with horror.

"Heaven help us!" Aunt Hyacinth had cried, her plump body slumping into a sofa. "Caroline! I am in need of my hartshorn!"

Caro had fled the room to return shortly with the hartshorn and her father.

"What on earth has occurred?" he had asked as he hurried into the room behind his daughter. "Caroline is rattling about you being accosted by some scoundrel."

She retold the story to him while Caro had tended to her near swooning mother.

Uncle Edmund, though a younger and smaller version of Uncle John, could still manage the legendary Allard glare when he was incensed.

"This is an outrage! I shall find out who this profligate is and have him horsewhipped," Uncle Edmund had stormed.

Sipping sweet tea, Julia had felt oddly comforted by her uncle's anger.

"Are you sure that he was dressed as a gentleman? I cannot believe anyone accepted in Polite Society could behave in such an unredeemable manner," Uncle Edmund had stated.

"Yes, Uncle, and the other men that were with him were all dressed very fashionably. In fact"—she had narrowed her gray eyes in concentration—"I believe his name is Kelbourne. Yes, that is it! One of the other men said that Kelbourne is confusing a vow with a wager."

She had sat back then, so pleased with herself for remembering the scoundrel's name that she did not immediately catch the thunderstruck expressions on her relatives' faces. Aunt Hyacinth's mouth had actually dropped open.

"You must be mistaken, Julia. The only Kelbourne I know of in Town is the *Duke* of Kelbourne. I cannot conceive . . ." Uncle Edmund's voice had trailed away as he and his wife had exchanged dismayed glances.

Aunt Hyacinth had looked at her husband with anguished eyes.

"Oh, Edmund! It could not possibly be the Duke of Kelbourne! Could it? I own he is a bit wild, but . . . Oh no! What if it is Kelbourne? The poor child will have to carry this with her, and the Season has barely started," she had cried.

Julia had looked at her aunt in growing alarm.

"If my niece cannot even stand on a London street

without being molested by some damned rakehell at three of the clock . . ."

The entrance of his son had interrupted Uncle Edmund's tirade. Roland Allard was a tall, handsome young man much like his father and known as quite a dasher around Town.

"I've just come from my club," Roland had stated without preamble. "I suspected that there could not be two lithe, lovely, *extremely tall*, flaxen-haired beauties unknown to the *ton* on Bolton Street today."

"Good Lord! Speak up, boy, tell us what you know," his father had urged.

"Well," he had begun in a hesitant voice before seating himself across from Julia, "I really am not privy to all the details. Unfortunately, Lord Torrington saw the whole thing happen. He had been at a celebration yesterday evening with the Kelbourne set. They were in high spirits because Kel, that is Kelbourne, had wagered a fortune on some untried pugilist in a match against Cooper."

"Pugilism! Never say Julia is somehow mixed up in pugilism," Aunt Hyacinth had said in horror.

"Not exactly, Mama," Roland had said.

Uncle Edmund had tossed an impatient glance to his wife. "Let the boy explain, Hyacinth."

Roland had continued. "Kelbourne's man somehow won the match in the wee hours. Everyone was there, and at the . . . er . . . celebration afterward Kel—and here is where my information gets sketchy—made some kind of vow."

"Yes, he did say something about not going back on a vow," Julia had interjected.

"Kelbourne, by all accounts made this vow publicly. Dame Fortune's name was invoked, and that caused all the blades and bucks to rush back to London and place wagers in the betting books of most of the clubs in Town," Roland had concluded.

"Good God," Uncle Edmund had expostulated.

"All I know is that by Kel's kissing Julia, enormous sums of money changed hands among a good number of the male members of the *ton* this afternoon."

"Oh dear." Caro had looked across to Julia with expressive eyes.

Julia had sat silent.

" 'Pon rep, Julia, I'd call Kelbourne out if I wasn't sure he'd put a hole through me," Roland had said, giving Julia a weak smile.

Uncle Edmund had jumped to his feet. "This is the most outrageous, unprincipled, insulting . . ." he had sputtered as he took long strides to the door. "Come, Roland, we shall pay a visit to Kelbourne this instant. I do not intend to let this jackanapes get away with this."

Roland had half risen to follow when his mother's voice halted them both.

"No, Edmund, you mustn't." Her voice had been authoritative despite the underlying note of panic.

Uncle Edmund had stopped mid-stride to look back at his wife in surprise.

"You do not expect me to let this insult to our niece pass?"

Julia had seen Aunt Hyacinth firm her lips. "Children, please leave so that your uncle and I can discuss this situation in private."

Julia and Caro had exchanged speaking looks before silently following Roland from the sitting room.

Breakfast the next morning had seemed to Julia like an odd and unpleasant dream.

Her uncle had not met her eyes once while Aunt Hyacinth went on about the weather in an overly cheerful tone of voice.

Roland had gulped his food and excused himself, throwing Julia a sympathetic look on the way out. Caro had said nothing and gazed at her mother in puzzlement. Julia had eaten very little, remained silent, and waited.

Finally, Aunt Hyacinth had set her cup down and looked across the table at Julia with the no-nonsense expression Julia had become very familiar with.

"My dear Julia, your uncle and I are aware of how important this Season is to you. But in light of yesterday's shocking occurrence, I feel—that is—your uncle and I feel that it would be in your best interest to postpone your come-out until the gossip dies down."

"Mama! You cannot mean it! Why, it is as if you are implying that somehow what happened yesterday was Julia's fault." Caro had stared at her mother in angry surprise.

"Not at all," Aunt Hyacinth had replied. "We are only speaking of a postponement. Do not take on so."

"But, Mama, this is not fair," Caro had continued her argument. "Papa, please tell Mama that Julia must stay!"

Julia had been touched by her cousin's loyalty and defense, but Julia also knew that her pleading would do no good.

"Perhaps it is for the best, because of the gossip . . ." Uncle Edmund's voice had trailed away on this feeble excuse.

"Who cares about the gossip! I want Julia to stay!" Caro had exclaimed.

Aunt Hyacinth had heaved a heavy sigh and folded her hands primly in her ample lap.

"Caro, you force me to be frank. Though we have a certain cachet among the *ton*, we certainly do not circulate to such heights as the Duke of Kelbourne. He is a nonpareil of the first consequence. The duke will not suffer a whit for accosting Julia on the street yesterday—but Julia will. Any number of people saw the event. Roland heard it being discussed in his club! If Julia appeared in Society, how long do you think it would take for her to be pointed at and gossiped about?''

This bit of logic had silenced Caro, and Julia could still recall the helpless, apologetic look on her cousin's face.

Julia had been sent back to Chippenham the very next day. All her friends and acquaintances had not even tried to hide their avid curiosity at her sudden return. The only person she had shared the truth with, other than Uncle John and Aunt Beryl, had been her lifelong friend, Miss Mariah Thorncroft.

Julia had found some comfort in her discussions with her friend, for Mariah had an equally vivid imagination when it came to dreaming up fitting punishments for the evil duke.

But even after a year, questions about her return still cropped up. Why, even Cynthia Arnold, a neighbor child she had taught to read, had asked Julia if she had been naughty in London. Again, she had been forced to fib—to a child—about why she had not stayed in London for the Season. How she hated the Duke of Kelbourne!

Sighing, Julia tried to push her frustrated, vengeful thoughts away. She suddenly became aware of the letter she held crumpled in her palm and decided to divert herself with the as yet unread letter from Caro.

Unfolding the paper, she pressed it to her knee to smooth some of the creases before reading it in the late afternoon light.

My Dearest Cousin,

I write this letter to beseech your company! Dear Julia, though I am a bride of only six months, I find that I must attend my mother-in-law in Bath, instead of going to London for the Season!

You know that I would never say a word to disagree with my darling Clive, but I believe that sometimes he is a trifle indulgent of his mama's megrims.

We have taken a house very near Lady Farren's, and Clive will not hear another word on the subject. But he does send his love to you and hopes you will come to Bath and stay with us. He knows how much your company delights me, and wishes that you would feel pity upon me and stay the entire summer. Was that not prettily put? Alas, I cannot be out of patience with my darling Clive for long.

As Chippenham is so close to Bath, your journey shall not be at all arduous. And unless I hear that you have the pox or something equally dreadful, I shall expect to see you on my doorstep within a fortnight.

I shall send you my direction in the next post. I hope my aunt and uncle Allard are well and are willing to share you with their bereft niece. Give them my love.

> *Your Loving,*
> *Caro*

Julia reread the letter with a growing smile. Indeed, she would seriously consider this unexpected invitation. Chippenham, especially after this last encounter with Mr. Fredericks, was having a stifling effect upon her of late. Her normal interests and pursuits had lost their appeal. She decided that Bath in the summer would be lovely.

Julia rose and left the lush garden. Entering the house from the wide stone steps that led to the French windows, she was aware of a budding sense of excitement, and was eager to discuss Caro's letter with her aunt and uncle.

The maid was just bringing the tea service into the

sitting room, where her relatives were enjoying the view of the front garden.

"Oh, good, you have come in. I was feeling much too lazy to go and fetch you for tea," Aunt Beryl called in a cheerful tone upon seeing her niece enter the room.

Julia smiled at her pretty, petite aunt as she seated herself in a comfortable chair across from her relatives. This was her favorite part of the day. To sit in this well-appointed room, with its warm, wood-paneled walls and myriad of cozy pillows, had always been a gentle pleasure.

Setting his newspaper aside, Uncle John looked at Julia with interest, his gray eyes very like her own. Of her deceased father's two brothers, Julia thought that Uncle John looked most like her papa.

"Was that Mr. Fredericks I saw going down the lane as if the hounds of Hades were on his heels?"

"Yes, it was. I believe that he will not be returning anytime soon," Julia sighed, and settled back comfortably in her chair.

"Oh no, Julia, not again!" her aunt cried, teapot suspended over her husband's cup. "I thought surely that he would not renew his proposal after the last time you declined him," she sighed, her still-brown curls shaking from beneath her mobcap.

"Yes, I am afraid that I had to speak quite plainly this time," Julia said, suppressing a lingering stab of guilt regarding Mr. Fredericks.

"Nonsense, m'dear. If he is so thickheaded that a simple *no* will not do, then he deserves to be sent off with a flea in his ear," Uncle John stated, accepting the cup from his wife.

Looking at her uncle with his shock of steel gray hair and erect military bearing, Julia decided to leave out the insult Mr. Fredericks had dealt her. Uncle

John would most likely call the younger man out if he knew.

"I have a letter from Caro," Julia said without preamble, "and she has invited me to go to Bath and stay with her for the summer."

At her aunt's and uncle's looks of surprise, she handed the letter across to Aunt Beryl.

While her aunt read the short missive, Julia sent a smile to her uncle. "I have not been away from Chippenham for some time. I have been rather dull lately, and I own a visit to Bath is appealing."

Uncle John frowned. "I do not know, Julia. The last time you went off from us, there was a spot of trouble."

Aunt Beryl snorted at this remark and laid the letter aside. "As if it was anyone's fault that cad accosted Julia. Really, John! It might do Julia a bit of good to be away from Chippenham for a while. It has been much too dull here. This last year, she has done nothing but help me in the garden or tutor some of the village children. Besides, Bath is not far—we could easily visit Julia and Caroline this summer. I certainly would not mind taking the waters."

A frown still creased her uncle's forehead, but he did not argue further with his wife or niece.

Sitting back in her chair with her steaming cup of tea, Julia's smile grew. Bath did indeed seem to be the perfect escape from unwanted suitors and nosy tabbies. She could not wait to send a note to Mariah Thorncroft with the news.

Chapter Two

The Duke of Kelbourne flicked aside another invitation, eyeing with distaste the growing pile on his desk. His secretary would be kept busy writing regrets, he mused. Leaning back in his leather chair, he gazed up at the hunting scene painted on the ceiling of his library for a moment before closing his eyes.

He found it curious, in a detached way, that though spring had arrived, he had not the least desire to go to his London townhouse and partake of the usual round of revelry with the other sprigs of the *ton*. He let this thought settle, lifted his legs, and placed his booted feet on his large desk, crossing his ankles.

For the last few weeks, he had been steadfast in his refusal to examine his reasons for not making any plans for the Season. Claiming that he had too many pressing issues to attend to at his country seat had sufficed for a while. But now his friends were beginning to badger him about going to London. After all, Mattonly had stressed in his most recent missive, the huge estate was constantly going through some sort of change or renovation and probably always would.

Some of his other friends had written to say that

the air in London was already crackling with the excitement of Princess Charlotte's impending wedding to Prince Leopold. Many amusements were set to honor the heir to the throne's nuptials, and Kel had invitations to every sort of soiree, levee, breakfast, and ball. He declined them all without a second glance.

However, Kel did find this avoidance of Town a shade out of his character. Since reaching his majority, the delights of the Season had always caused his pulse to quicken. Though he loved Kelbourne Keep, after a long winter he was usually so restless he could not wait to go to Town and kick up his heels. Even during the war, there had been enough excitement in Town to keep him there for the whole Season.

But not this year. Even his duties at Parliament could not compel him to leave his home. Shifting in his chair to a more comfortable slouch, he tried to bestir himself into some sort of interest for the allures of Town. All his friends were there. Racing, boxing, and fencing kept him busy. He waited for a reaction. Nothing. Not even the slightest lifting of this dashed ennui.

Puckering his brows, he tried again. He enjoyed the opera and the theater, and every Season there was at least one amusing bit of muslin that held his attention for a while. Again, nothing.

How about gambling? High stakes were sure to liven up an evening. Ah, finally, his pulse stirred at the thought of gambling. A good wager never failed to get his blood up. He had not had a good gamble since the beginning of last Season.

Last Season. It was not the thought of gambling that caused his pulse to stir; it was the thought of that last wager in particular.

With a quick movement, he lowered his legs,

pushed himself up from his desk, grabbed his walking stick, and headed for the French doors in the main salon. He strode out onto the terraced balcony that led to the garden and parkland beyond.

With long strides, he ambled over his land, eating up yards without any real notion of a destination. The day was glorious and warm, reminding him of that other glorious spring day, last year in London.

When *she* had stepped out of the shop, the sun shining on her exquisite face, he had stopped dead on the sidewalk. It was odd how now, almost one year later, he could still recall certain aspects of the scene without any difficulty.

He remembered that she was very tall, that her expressive eyes were a clear, true gray, and that she wore a gray gown. That gray gown and the fact that she appeared to be unattended caused him to conclude that the Beauty was probably some poor abigail on an errand.

He realized that everything in his well-ordered world had changed that day. At first, he was not aware that the event had had any effect upon him. He had waited for everything to return to normal— but it had not. Town had palled quickly, and he had returned to Kelbourne Keep, his principal seat, well before the Season was over.

Leaving the lush formality of his garden, he walked over an ornamental stone bridge and entered the extensive, rolling parkland with the vague notion of going to the lake some distance away.

It had taken until last Christmas to realize that he was feeling an emotion he could not recall having experienced since childhood. Shame.

He clearly recalled the moment this realization came to him. The entire extended Wenlock family had been enjoying a festive Christmas dinner. Halfway through the meal, something in the way Emmaline, his older sister, smiled had caught his attention. Her pleased expression had reminded him of the Beauty.

The thought that followed had hit him like a blow to the chest. How would he feel if a man had treated his sister the way he had treated that young woman on the street that day?

For the previous seven months he had tried to keep this realization at bay by telling himself that his only intention had been an innocent kiss to honor Dame Fortune. But on Christmas day, as he sat at the head of his table with his family around him, a deep shame washed over him.

He was a gentleman not only by birth and rank, but also by the teachings and examples of his own father and mother. At his dinner table that day, with his family completely unaware of his inner turmoil, he finally owned that accosting the young woman, even for an *innocent* kiss, had been beneath him as a gentleman.

Though the long-denied emotion still stung, he had felt a little better for accepting that he had done wrong. But this new self-awareness had only gone so far to assuage the deadly mood that had been his companion for nigh on a year.

He reached the lake and, with a pleasant sense of fatigue, decided to remove his coat and rest on a massive boulder at the water's edge. Though the boulder appeared upon the land as if placed there by nature, it, like the lake, had been designed by his landscape architect, Humphrey Repton. Kel was very satisfied with the change in the terrain, and it had solved some of the flooding problems another part of the estate had been experiencing for generations.

Tossing his walking stick aside, he drew one booted foot up onto the boulder, and rested his forearm upon his knee. Maybe Emmaline and Maman were right—they were always after him to marry and plan for the next generation.

After all, he would be thirty in August. Was marriage the answer? he wondered. Maybe it was—he certainly had the perfect wife in mind. Maman had long ago chosen Lady Davinia Harwich to be his future bride.

Lord Harwich's land, a sizable estate, marched with the Keep. The earl had made it clear that he had no issue with dowering his estate to his only daughter, as the title and other property were entailed to his nephew.

Marriage to the elegant Davinia had always been in the back of Kel's mind, but it now seemed like something he should bring to the forefront.

Besides, Kelbourne Keep needed a mistress, he thought, warming to the idea.

He watched the swans feeding on the placid lake for some time, feeling soothed by the warmth radiating from the boulder. Turning his head a little, he looked across the distance to Kelbourne Keep.

Beautifully situated on a massive rise, the Keep had a commanding view of the Vale of Kelbourne. His heart swelled, as it always did, when seeing his home from this vantage point.

Since the reign of Edward the Confessor, the Wenlocks, lords of Kelbourne, had wielded great power in this part of the country. Though the last few generations of Wenlocks were soldiers and statesmen, his ancestors had been feudal warriors—or, as his grandmother liked to put it more delicately, "men of a martial inclination."

A slight smile came to his lips at this as he continued to survey his home. During his childhood, he had spent many carefree days exploring the vast estate. But since inheriting the title, long before he expected to bear such responsibility, he had developed a love and appreciation of his home that was as deep as it was rarely expressed.

As a young man he had traveled to the Continent and the Mediterranean, finding great pleasure in the beauty of ancient places. He had filled numerous sketchbooks with his attempts to capture some of his favorite sights. But nothing he had seen in his travels had ever compared to the majestic turrets of iron gray stone and the sweeping view of the Vale from his ancestral home.

Suddenly, he was aware that he felt much more the thing. The Keep and all the other Kelbourne holdings needed to be protected for the future. He now saw his duty clearly: it was time for a change in his life.

Rising, he picked up his jacket, flung it over his shoulder, and retrieved his walking stick from the ground. In no hurry, he made his way back to the Keep. He would call on Lord Harwich in the next few days, he decided, and begin paying court to Lady Davinia.

He felt better for having formulated a plan, and arrived back at his library in much improved spirits.

It was still several hours before dinner, so he decided to finish attending to the correspondence he had abandoned earlier.

The last letter in the stack was from his sister, he was pleased to see, and broke the seal quickly.

Dear Kel,

I trust this letter finds you well. I was surprised to see from your last letter that you have not yet opened your house in Town. But I am hoping that you will delay the Season a little longer and immediately attend me in Bath.

I shall be blunt: Maman and Grandmère are driving me to distraction. You notice I say your mother

*and grandmother. I do not claim them as kin this
fortnight.*

*Maman is being impossibly stubborn, and
Grandmère is being annoyingly imperious. I knew
from the start that it would be a challenging proposition for the three of us to share a house this summer.
But spring is not even spent, and the two of them
are already at daggers drawn.*

*Again, I beg that you come to Bath and attend this
situation, Kel. Maman will not take another house,
Grandmère will not leave either, and I cannot leave
for fear that they shall fight like cat and dog. You
know you are the only one either of them listens to,
so please be a dear and come rescue me from your
relatives. I told you I do not presently claim them.*

*Besides, I have not seen you since Christmas, and
I own your company would do us all some good.*

*I must close as I hear Maman and Gran arguing
over the tea, of all things. Please say you will come.
The waters here do not seem to be helping either of
their tempers.*

*Your loving sister,
Emmaline*

The duke folded the letter and sat back with a
slight frown. He had wondered how long it would
take to receive a letter like this. In truth, he had not
expected it this soon.

After last Christmas, when Emmaline had informed him that she would be staying with Maman
and Grandmère, their paternal grandmother, he had
thought she was joking.

"Oh, Kel, they are both past their old, petty grievances toward each other," Emma had assured him.
"Besides, it's silly for them to have separate houses

in Bath, and expect me to go back and forth visiting them. This is the logical solution.''

But the duke knew better. Maman and Grandmère had never gotten on well, and he could not imagine them doing so now. In spite of Emma's dry-humored letter, he knew she loathed bickering and tension. Since losing her husband, Charles, Emmaline's temperament was not as strong as it used to be.

Pulling a penknife from the desk drawer, the duke began to sharpen the nib of his quill. He had no doubt that his sister would be pleased by his letter informing her that she should expect to see him within the week.

Putting the female contingency of his family in a good humor would be the easiest thing in the world to do—he had only to inform them of his plans to marry. That would divert them from their nonsense quickly enough, he mused with a slight smile as he put quill to paper.

Chapter Three

*T*wo days before her intended departure for Bath, Julia set out to visit her childhood friend, Mariah Thorncroft.

As she walked through the creaking garden gate, Julia looked back at the home she had treasured since early childhood. Her aunt and uncle had always proudly tended the simple yet spacious two-story brick house, and it showed. Seen from the superior vantage point of the lane, the sight of her aunt's flourishing garden never failed to stir Julia's heart.

In a purposeful fashion, Julia walked along the narrow road. She carried several books, and her bonnet dangled from her arm by its peach-colored ribbons, which matched her simple muslin gown. The day was warm, and the sunbeams dodging through the tree branches felt good upon her face. Her booted feet made a satisfying crunch on the cobbles as her long strides ate up the distance.

Fledgling birds sang overhead, and Julia smiled at the sight of purple clematis growing next to a twisted oak on the side of the road. With a feeling of delight, she reveled at the evidence of spring all around her.

The walk to Mariah's house was always one Julia enjoyed, and she took pleasure in every familiar turn and rise in the road. She loved the village, too, and recalled with amusement how frightened she had been when she had first arrived at her aunt and uncle's home.

Her papa had brought her to stay soon after her mama had died. Julia had mounted the front steps with trepidation, clutching her father's hand. Aunt Beryl had opened the door and immediately enveloped her in a secure and warm embrace.

"My, aren't you a tall girl for only being five years old," was the first thing Julia remembered her aunt saying.

After the dim, sickroom atmosphere of her parents' home, life with her aunt and uncle could not have been more different. They allowed her to run, yell, and visit with other children. Aunt Beryl read to her and taught her to sew. Uncle John also spent time with her when he was not away on military duties. He took her fishing and taught her how to draw a bow so the arrow would fly straight and true. They both had always made her feel as if she were their own.

Over the years, her papa would visit occasionally. He had been a quiet man, and looking back, Julia believed he had not the slightest notion of what to do with a little girl.

Sadly, he had been killed in one of the early battles of the war with France. His death had been upsetting, although not as devastating as it would have been had they been closer.

It was not only her deep love for her aunt and uncle, but her profound gratitude for taking her in that caused her to strive to be the very best daughter she could be. The feeling of wanting to be perfect for her aunt and uncle was another reason why her abrupt return from London galled so badly.

She still thanked the good Lord every Sunday that

Uncle John had been returned to them unhurt. Unlike any number of other soldiers who came back from the war, he was fortunate to have no financial worries. Showing much wisdom as a younger man, he had invested money from an inheritance in a sugarcane plantation in Jamaica.

Over the years he had reinvested the profits in various ventures, mostly successful. There was no need to live on a retired soldier's half-pay, and he was known throughout the district as a very generous man.

Though ostensibly raised as an only child, for her aunt and uncle had not been blessed with their own children, Julia had never been lonely. There had often been long visits with her cousins and various other family members. She had also formed an early, and lasting, friendship with Mariah Thorncroft.

When she reached the age of eighteen, her aunt and uncle had given her a grand reception in lieu of a Season. John and Beryl had little fondness for Town, therefore, Julia had no desire to go there either.

After that, several young men had approached her uncle about paying court to her, but as she had little affection for any of them, her uncle had discouraged their suits.

Over the years Aunt Beryl had helped shape Julia's opinion on marriage.

"My dear, it is not as it was a hundred years ago. We live in much more enlightened times. There is no reason for an intelligent girl from a good family to feel constrained to marry anyone. I was almost eight-and-twenty before I met your uncle. If we had not met, I would have never married, and would have thought nothing of it," Aunt Beryl had told her.

So Julia had continued to reside in her relatives' home, happy and secure with her lot. But over time, as she had left her ungainly girlishness behind, the gentlemen in the district had begun to display the oddest reactions to her looks.

At the local assemblies, they would stare to the point of gawking. Or they would stammer and stutter over silly attempts at poetry extolling her beauty. She had grown quite accustomed to these awkward responses to her appearance, and they had even afforded amusement on some occasions.

Though village life was generally quiet, there was a considerable amount of social activity in the area. The Thorncrofts entertained, as did Squire Heath. The Allards were also noted for their laughter-filled gatherings, though Aunt Beryl enjoyed society much more than her husband did. He preferred to ensconce himself in his library with his cronies while his wife and niece entertained.

It was not until Caro and Aunt Hyacinth had sent her numerous letters rhapsodizing over the delights of a London Season that Julia had started to consider leaving Chippenham for the spring.

And what a short trip it had turned out to be!

It was rather amusing that Aunt Hyacinth now wanted her to return to London. Her aunt had started a campaign of letters at the beginning of the year. Julia had received one from her aunt every week for the last three months.

Now that Caro was safely married, and Julia's smudged reputation could no longer reflect badly upon her cousin, Aunt Hyacinth was eager to make up the lost Season to Julia.

She also suspected that Aunt Hyacinth had so enjoyed arranging her daughter's come-out, she wanted to have the fun all over again with Julia. In her last letter, Aunt Hyacinth had been on the verge of pleading with Julia to come to London. The letter had gone on for pages about how exciting London was, due to Princess Charlotte's engagement. Romance was in the air, Aunt Hyacinth had extolled.

Without hesitaton Julia had gently declined her aunt's invitations. London no longer held any appeal for her, Princess Charlotte's engagement or not.

As Julia walked on, she wondered how many times she had taken this route to her friend's home. Hundreds and hundreds, she guessed. After all, she and Mariah had been close friends for almost twenty years and had been visiting each other since girlhood.

The Thorncrofts lived in a grand house on the knoll at the end of this two-mile lane. Mrs. Thorncroft had a passion for improving Thorncroft Manor, as she had styled the large estate. Her husband, the most prosperous woolen mill owner in the district, happily indulged his wife's continual demands to refurbish the place. All of the best families in Chippenham were invited to the Thorncrofts' home every year after the sheepshearing was done. It pleased Mrs. Thorncroft to no end to have her neighbors marvel as she unveiled the latest improvement to the Manor. Often Mariah would visit the Allards just to find relief from the hammering and dust that seemed a constant state at her house.

Julia was within half a mile of the Thorncrofts' when she saw Mariah's familiar figure coming toward her in the distance.

As if in accord, both young ladies hurried their steps toward one another with smiles of greeting.

Mariah Thorncroft was a lovely young woman with sparkling eyes and glorious wavy brown hair. As she drew near, Julia admired her friend's elegant sea-foam green walking gown. This was not unusual, as Mariah always dressed in the highest kick of fashion. The shawl she wore at her elbows was a marvel of intricately embroidered flowers. Julia had long thought Mariah was the perfect height—tall enough to be considered fashionable, but not so tall as to be remarked upon. Julia envied her friend's shorter stature and often told her so.

"Julia! I vow I left the house when you left yours, but as your strides are so much longer than mine, it takes you half the time to cover the same distance." Mariah Thorncroft's hazel eyes danced with an ever-present tease for her friend.

With her free hand, Julia reached out and clasped the other girl's arm with great affection.

"My dear Mariah, you have used that excuse for years. I think it is more likely that you stand looking out an attic window until I come into sight, *then* you leave your home," she teased back.

"I shall never admit to it," Mariah said, giving Julia's arm an answering squeeze as they stood in the middle of the lane. "What shall we do today?"

"As it is so fine outside, I thought a walk to the village would do us both good. And, I have these books that should be returned to the lending library," she suggested. "We can also go to Fitch's and see how Johnny Potts is getting on in his new position."

"Oh, let's. I am so proud of him. I know he will blush scarlet when he sees us, but will be pleased nonetheless."

Julia agreed. For the last six or seven years, Julia and Mariah had taken it upon themselves to teach some of the children in the village rudimentary requirements of reading, writing, and sums.

Johnny Potts, the youngest son of a poor sheep farmer, had turned out to be their prize pupil. Though he had at first been embarrassed and self-effacing at being instructed by women, over time he had flourished under their gentle guidance.

Recently, Julia and Mariah had each received a

note from Johnny, in his very careful and precise handwriting, informing them that he had been offered a position at Fitch's Mercantile. His gratitude had been deeply touching, and it had fueled the two young ladies' desire to instruct any child who had the desire, but not the means, to learn.

"Oh, I have not told you the latest news from my home," Mariah offered. "Mama is having the workmen start on her latest project. I have been combating the headache all day," Mariah said, slipping her arm through her friend's.

The two young women turned and left the lane, taking a wider road that led to High Street.

"What is your mama having done now?" Julia asked in sympathy as she shortened her stride to better match her friend's steps.

Mariah gave a heavy, exasperated sigh. "She has decided that nothing will do but to have a Greek temple overlooking the pond. Thank heavens the architect convinced her that a full-scale temple might overshadow the Manor. So we are to have a diminutive marble temple to lounge in."

"A Greek temple?" Julia tried to picture such a thing with the Thorncrofts' half-timbered Tudor mansion in the background. She could not. "Oh my. How long will it take to be completed?"

"The answer to that question is the only good thing about Mama's mania for improvements. The architect says it may take two years, since the marble is coming all the way from Italy. Papa says she cannot start on another scheme before this one is completed."

"What an undertaking! You must visit my aunt and uncle often to give yourself a respite from all the noise."

"I shall certainly take advantage of your aunt's and

uncle's hospitality," Mariah stated cheerfully. "Any news since I saw you last week?"

Julia stopped and looked down at her friend with an expression of annoyance mixed with amusement. "Yes, there is. You will never guess who proposed to me again, and then was astoundingly rude."

"Oh no! Not Mr. Fredericks again," Mariah said on a disbelieving laugh.

Julia gave her friend all the details of her awkward encounter with their neighbor.

"How horrible of him to suggest that there is something unseemly about your return from London. In truth, I suspect it is Widow March spreading this gossip about you—she casts sheep's eyes at Mr. Fredericks every Sunday and is jealous that he is so obvious about his preference of you. Still, I shall tell Mama that he is no longer welcome to tea," Mariah stated, the anger evident in her expressive eyes.

"There is no need to do that, Mariah. To give him the cut will only cause more talk. I have determined to treat him with the utmost civility when next we meet."

"Your tolerance is to be admired, dear Julia. I would not be so sanguine in your position. But I do envy your poise," Mariah said as they resumed their stroll toward the village.

"I lose what poise I have at the thought of the Duke of Kelbourne. It has been a year, and still his actions plague me. Mr. Fredericks' insult is a direct result of the duke accosting me."

"Yes, it is. The Duke of Kelbourne should be boiled in oil," Mariah proclaimed loyally.

The two young ladies had spent a good deal of time over the last year planning different, tortuous ways to end the existence of the dastardly duke. Boiling in oil had become a recent favorite.

"Indeed. But regarding Mr. Fredericks, I am grateful that my aunt and uncle have not placed any pressure on me to marry a man like him. I know some in the village would think me a goose-cap for rejecting the suit of a man with his income."

"I so envy you in that respect. As a woman of means, you have no need to marry unless you have a true regard for the gentleman."

Her gray eyes wide with surprise, Julia stopped short and looked at her friend. She grew more concerned when she took in her friend's serious expression.

"Envy me? Dearest Mariah, what fustian is this? I own that my father left me in no fear of the poorhouse, but my six hundred pounds a year does not compare with the enormity of your dowry. Your papa is the wealthiest man in the district. What reason do you have to envy me on this account?"

Mariah raised her tilted hazel eyes to Julia's face, seeking understanding. "Yes, my papa has settled a fortune upon me, but I have no money of my own."

As they continued to walk, Julia mulled over her friend's bald statement. "Oh, Mariah."

"My mama makes sure I am the most fashionably and expensively dressed young lady in the village," Mariah said in a tight voice. "But I cannot pay for my own subscription to the lending library. I cannot even purchase a sweet in the village today, for I have not a sou of my own. I have asked papa for a little pin money, but he prefers to have even the smallest bill sent to him. He believes that women cannot really understand the value of money and likes to know where every tuppence goes. Yes, my friend, I do envy you."

"In truth, everyone knows that your papa is exceedingly careful with his money, but I had no idea it was this bad! Why have you not shared this with me before?" Julia was at a loss as to what else to say and could only listen with sympathy and acceptance.

"What is the use?" Mariah shrugged, her lips twisting into a bitter smile. "I only tell you now because I am distraught at the thought of returning to London for the Season. Mama is determined to continue her hunt for a husband for me. She wants the highest title Papa's money can buy. I hate the thought of returning to London. It will be as awful as it was last year after you left. Now you are going to Bath, and Mama will drag me to Town. It will be awful all over again."

They walked in silence for several minutes. A cackling crow flew above their heads.

With anxiety, Julia sought for something she could say to give some comfort. Her heart twisted at hearing the anguish in her friend's voice. Though it was common knowledge that Mrs. Thorncroft was a shameless social climber, Julia had no idea the situation was so serious.

Suddenly, she stopped short and turned to her friend in great excitement, almost dropping her books. "I have an idea! Bath is certainly not as fashionable as London, but it has something London does not."

"What?" Mariah asked, a slight glimmer of hope entering her eyes.

"My cousin Caroline," Julia stated, waiting for her friend to see where she was leading.

"Your cousin Caroline? I am quite fond of Caro, but I do not . . . ?"

"She is Lady Farren now!" Julia interrupted in a tumble of words. "Do not you see? Now that Caro is a baroness, she can provide you with superior company. Your mama will scramble at the chance to be taken up by Lady Farren. Instead of going to London again with the hope that some titled gentleman will stumble across you, you can come to Bath! We must make it sound as enticing as possible for your mama."

Dawning understanding and excitement spread across Mariah's heart-shaped face as she took in the words. "Do you really think Mama might change our plans?"

"It is certainly worth a try. I shall write to Caro this day. I have complete confidence that you shall receive an invitation to one of her parties. Your mama is sure to see the advantage of an invitation from Lady Farren. Besides, we are less than two hours from Bath, which is another advantage. You must begin cajoling your mama this very afternoon. I know how stubborn you can be. Dig your heels in! Tell her it is Bath or nothing," Julia said, smiling, pleased to see the hint of hope on her friend's face.

"I shall!" Mariah vowed with sudden resolve. "Mama will see that this is a much better plan than going to London in such a haphazard manner. If we go to Bath, we shall already have an entrée into Society. You are brilliant! I feel ever so much better," she said with relief and excitement as they resumed their walk toward the village.

"I believe this spring will be much better than the last. For both of us," Julia said, with a nod of satisfaction.

Chapter Four

$\mathcal{A}$ light rain had cooled the day, making the fourteen-mile trip from Chippenham to Bath a pleasant experience for Julia and her maid, Harper.

As the carriage trundled to a stop, Julia looked out the window and saw Caroline waiting on the wide front steps of an impressive Palladian-style townhouse.

"Julia! You are here! Welcome, welcome," Caro called as she descended the marble stone steps.

With excited impatience, Julia opened the door before the footman had time to reach the coach. As the manservant helped her down, she was careful to lift the hem of her mauve carriage dress clear of a puddle.

Safely on the walkway, Julia beamed at her cousin and was much pleased to see how well she looked. Caro had always been pretty, but there was a new maturity in her expression and manner of dress that Julia thought suited her splendidly.

"Caro, you are a vision," Julia stated as they met in a warm embrace.

Pulling back, Caroline slipped her arm through Julia's, and led her up the steps. "Thank you, dear cousin. I vow your beauty shall soon be setting Bath on its ear. But for now we must make you comfortable. I have tea awaiting us in the salon. Clive fully intended to be at my side to greet you, but his mama sent a note over saying she was feeling poorly and needed his company."

Julia could not help noticing how flat Caro's voice had become. Looking at her closely as they entered the well-appointed foyer, Julia decided not to pretend that all was well.

"Is Lord Farren's mama a true thorn in your side?" she asked in gentle tones.

Caroline did not answer immediately, but continued to lead her across the entryway to the salon. Once there, Julia noticed the tea tray on a nearby table and began removing her doeskin gloves and bonnet.

As they sat down, Caro sighed deeply before beginning to prepare the tea.

"I shall confess to you that Lady Farren puts me out of all patience," she said, handing a teacup and saucer to her cousin. "At first, her demands upon Clive were not so noticeable—but now he goes to her townhouse almost daily."

"Oh my," Julia said, thinking how she would feel in the same circumstances.

Rattling her teaspoon with more force than necessary, Caroline continued. "Please do not misunderstand me—she is not at all mean. It is just that she behaves as if I am a little girl beneath her notice. She even refers to me as 'the girl,' and takes it as a matter of course that Clive will discard whatever plans we have to wait upon her. In truth, I am peeved at him for not being here when you arrived. It is not like him to be rude, and I do not like it."

Setting her cup down, Julia reached across the settee and grasped her cousin's hand. "Oh my dear! This must be very difficult. Your letters have contained a tone of humor on the subject of your mama-in-law, but I have suspected that something was amiss underneath. Forgive me for being blunt, but have you no influence over your husband?"

"Dear Julia, do not apologize for your bluntness—we have always been so with one another. But to your point, no, I have little influence over Clive when it comes to his mama. You see, I believe I have made a mistake in how I have handled my husband."

"What do you mean?" Julia asked as she retrieved her tea and leaned back against the cushions.

"I was so besotted with him the first few months of our marriage that it never occurred to me that he would not feel the same. I was the most accommodating, understanding, insipid bride there ever was. You would have thought me such a pea goose."

"Caro, you are too harsh with yourself."

"Not at all, even my mama said so. But after a short time, I became just the opposite. I began to demand that he spend more time with me. I complained dreadfully about the time he spends with his mother. Lady Farren makes everything so pleasant for him that I believe he found it a relief to be at her house. He chided me about how his understanding wife had disappeared. When I confided in Mama, she said I must begin flirting and teasing him. That I must become cunning and devise ways to bring him to my side as his mother does." Caro's expression showed distaste of her mother's advice.

"That certainly sounds like Aunt Hyacinth," Julia said with a wry expression.

"But I do not want to behave that way! That is another reason I am so pleased that you are staying with us. If I am to be neglected, then I shall have my dearest cousin to keep me company. And do not be alarmed by what I have said, you shall not regret coming to Bath. We are going to have a lovely time—

and tomorrow I shall take you to sign the subscription books at the assembly rooms, though I only attend the Upper Room. We shall go this Thursday eve whether Clive escorts us or not," Caro finished with a decisive nod.

Julia watched her cousin in silence for a moment. Though she wore her brown hair in a more sophisticated style and the missish gowns she used to wear were gone, Julia realized with a bit of a pang that Caro was a very young two-and-twenty.

"Enough of my grumbles. Pray tell me, how are my aunt and uncle Allard?"

"They are extremely fit and send their love," Julia replied, willing to let the troublesome subject of her cousin's mother-in-law drop for the moment. "Uncle John was not in wholehearted agreement with my coming to Bath. But Aunt Beryl and I presented a united front, and he had to give in."

Caro smiled at this, the stress in her blue eyes easing a bit. "I have sent them an invitation to the soiree I am giving at the end of the month. I do hope they will come."

"I shall follow your invitation with a letter of my own. I am sure I shall be missing them by then," Julia replied.

"Oh, I almost forgot. I have sent an invitation to the Thorncrofts also. Poor Mariah! I vow she must be a changeling, she has so little resemblance to her mama."

"How do you mean? I have always thought Mariah and Mrs. Thorncroft somewhat resembled each other," she said with a curious frown.

"Well, mayhap in *appearance*, but not at all in manner. I saw Mariah and Mrs. Thorncroft last year in London—after Mama and Papa were so dreadful and sent you home." Her cousin's tone held a hint of old anger.

"Now, Caro, we have gone over this dozens of times. I understand perfectly why I could not continue in London. It is the fault of that beastly duke, and no one else's. Now, go on about Mariah and her mother."

"Well, all right," Caro said with a moue. "Mariah is so gentle and funny, with such a sense of understanding and delicacy. But Mrs. Thorncroft is the opposite. We, of course, invited them to our at-homes and parties and such. There, Mrs. Thorncroft would gush and coo about how rich they are, how generous a dowry Mariah has. Poor Mariah would be beet red even if she were on the other side of the room. It was apparent to the *ton* that Mrs. Thorncroft was a mushroom. No one else took them up."

Julia looked thoughtful. "No wonder she was dreading the thought of returning to London for another Season."

"I do hope they come. Bath is not as dull as it is reputed to be."

"Mariah would tell you she does not care if Bath is as dull as dishwater."

Caro smiled, and silence held them for a bit as they finished their tea.

Setting her cup back on the tray, Caroline looked at Julia. "Now, would you like to walk, or would you rather rest?"

"Walk, please. I am not in the least tired, and would love to see a bit of the area. It has been years since I was last here."

"Lady Farren says that it is becoming too crowded. You should see how she elbows lesser-ranked mortals out of her way in the Pump Room," Caro said with a little laugh.

Sensing a lingering bitterness under her cousin's light tone, Julia gave her an encouraging smile.

"I believe you are correct, Caro dear. We shall have

a lovely time this summer," she said to divert the conversation to more pleasant matters.

Caroline looked at Julia with an anxious frown. "You are not just saying that? After all, now that I am married, Mama would love to sponsor a proper come-out for you in London. The gossip about you is long past. I know she has written to tell you so."

"Yes, Aunt Hyacinth has invited me to London, but I would much rather be here with you. Besides, if I ever saw the Duke of Kelbourne again, I might not be able to resist the urge to shoot him."

Leaning against the back of the settee, Caroline laughed aloud. "We cannot have that! Much better that you are here with me."

By Thursday, while preparing for her evening out, Julia decided that accepting Caro's invitation had been a capital idea. Bath, being much larger than Chippenham, offered any number of amusing entertainments. Caro had taken her on several excursions around town, and Julia enjoyed browsing through establishments that boasted a wider array of goods than what she was accustomed to at home.

She had also met several of Caro's friends and found that she liked her cousin's husband more than she thought she would. Lord Farren was the epitome of politeness, and cut quite a dashing figure with his tall, slim figure and boyish shock of blond hair.

He had apologized profusely at dinner the first night for not being there to greet her when she arrived.

"You see, my mother has been unwell, and she quite depends on me to attend her occasionally," he had explained with an offhand air.

Julia had dismissed his concern and assured him that she understood. But she noticed the harried glances he often threw to Caro and wondered if her cousin's husband was more aware of his wife's ire than he let on.

A knock at the door interrupted her reflections, and Harper, her maid, entered. She carried a gown draped across her outstretched arms.

"The creases came out completely, miss," Harper stated with satisfaction as she laid the rose pink evening dress across the bed.

Turning sideways on her vanity chair, Julia was pleased to see the silk was indeed void of wrinkles. It was one of her favorite gowns, and she loved the dozens of seed pearls embroidered into the little puffed sleeves. She felt the gown gave her an air of elegance, and had decided earlier that it would be the perfect choice to make her first appearance in Bath society.

She smiled at the maid in appreciation. "Thank you, Harper."

Turning back to the mirror, she picked up a pair of seed pearl earbobs and affixed them to her lobes. Harper went to the wardrobe on the other side of the pretty, spacious bedchamber and began collecting the slippers, shawl, and reticule to complete Julia's ensemble.

"I hope I am not in danger of being late." Julia took a piece of chamois and carefully dipped it into a little pot of finely milled French powder and pressed it to her nose and forehead.

"No, miss, you have time enough to get ready at your leisure," Harper said as she finished laying out the accessories.

Julia did take her time with her toilette. A little while later, when she was dressed and Harper was putting the final touches on her upswept hair, Julia was quite satisfied with her appearance.

After bidding farewell to her maid, she left the bedchamber to meet her cousin in the foyer. She was giving her gloves a last tug when she heard the deep tones of a masculine voice.

Looking down into the foyer below, Julia was surprised to see Lord Farren, resplendent in evening dress, waiting with his wife. Caro looked up and smiled her delight at Julia.

"Look! My Lord Farren has decided to escort us this evening! Is that not gallant of him?"

With an answering smile, Julia completed her descent. When she reached the bottom of the stairs, she could not help noticing Lord Farren's flushed cheeks as he greeted her. His wife's profuse praise had embarrassed him, she surmised with secret amusement.

"I shall be lauded the luckiest fellow in Bath to be in the company of two Incomparables," he stated.

Julia curtsied in response to his compliment. The butler then made the pronouncement that the carriage had been brought around.

Following Caro and Clive out to the front steps, Julia felt her pulse begin to quicken. She had to admit that she was rather excited at the prospect of dancing in a ballroom. The assemblies and impromptu dances in Chippenham were smallish affairs, and she had not been in London long enough to attend any large parties, so this evening would be a new experience.

Settling in across from the Farrens as the coach set off, Julia smiled as Caro chattered away. It was obvious that she was inordinately pleased with her husband's company. Julia was happy for her cousin and hoped that this would be the beginning of a new closeness for the newly wed couple.

Some minutes later, Julia looked out the window, and saw a line of carriages pulling up to the elegant, understated entryway of the establishment. Despite her impatience, she resisted the urge to get out and walk the rest of the way. From her short acquaintance with Lord Farren, she knew he was a high stickler when it came to the niceties.

By the time a lackey opened the coach door, Julia and Caro were both tapping their feet with eagerness.

When they all had exited the carriage, Lord Farren offered each lady an arm and escorted them through the entryway and into the anteroom. Once there, Julia took in the other guests. The chatter and the array of finery on display added to her feeling of excited anticipation. As the three of them inched their way closer to the doors leading to the ballroom, numerous people greeted Lord and Lady Farren.

Putting her hand to her brow for a moment, Julia looked around in growing concern. She was beginning to feel a bit oppressed by the crush surging toward the ballroom. But once in, the room seemed to open up before her and was less crowded. Relieved, she glanced around the immense oblong space. Instantly, she was impressed with the ballroom's size and design. Graceful Corinthian-style pilasters lined the walls, as if upholding them. Her eyes traveled upward to the five superb chandeliers hanging from the coved ceiling, their countless candles casting a festive glow over the assemblage.

Again, a current of excitement raced up her arms as she gazed at her impressive surroundings. The prospect of being somewhere new and in different company added to her pleasure.

"If you will notice behind you, there is a recessed loft for the musicians." Lord Farren directed her attention to a semicircular alcove set high above the dancers.

"How clever and elegantly done," Julia said.

Moving farther into the room behind Caro, Julia saw that although there was a predominance of older people, there did seem to be enough younger people to keep the evening from becoming dull.

Almost at once, other guests came forward and surrounded them. Soon, Julia was being introduced to so many people, she knew she would never be able to recall all their names.

There was little time to converse, for at that moment the Master of Ceremonies was arranging to lead the highest-ranking lady onto the floor. Caro diverted Julia's attention by leaning up to her and whispering from behind her fan. "Every unattached gentleman in the room is casting his eyes your way—and a few of the married ones, too."

Julia's face remained impassive. Using the guise of readjusting her shawl, she surreptitiously glanced around the crowded room. Somewhat to her surprise, there were several gentlemen looking in her direction.

"You may be right, but unfortunately, most of them are at least two inches shorter than I," she whispered back.

"Oh, you may scoff, but by the end of the evening you will be the rage of Bath."

Before Julia could respond to this prediction, Lord Farren stepped forward to claim his wife's hand. "Come, Caroline, we are to make up the numbers."

Hastily, Caro introduced Julia to a Mrs. Crowley, before happily going off with her husband.

Soaring music of a lively country dance filled the expanse as Julia stood with Mrs. Crowley, an agreeable young matron, exchanging pleasantries and watching the dancers perform the figures.

From the corner of her eye, her attention was caught by a familiar female figure weaving her way through the throng toward her. Julia's heart sank. She was not surprised to see Harriett March; she knew the widow had relatives in Bath. But she was surprised the widow would approach her. Mrs. March, an attractive woman a few years older than she, had never been very friendly. And since Julia's unexplained return from London last year, the widow had not been shy in publicly questioning the reason Julia had not stayed in London.

There seemed to be no way of avoiding this unappealing encounter.

"La, but I thought my eyes had hoaxed me! It is Miss Julia Allard. Fancy seeing you here in Bath."

Julia turned and looked down upon the fair-haired woman. "Good evening, Mrs. March."

"What brings you here to Bath, Miss Allard? Alas, this sedate town has always been a favored spot for young ladies to live down a scandal. But, of course, I am sure that is not why *you* have come to Bath," she ended with a titter, flipping her fan open with a snap.

Pausing to collect her composure, Julia forced herself to smile at the petite, blond woman. Aware that Mrs. Crowley was attending the conversation, she spoke in even tones.

"I am visiting my cousin, Lady Farren." Maybe if she refused to respond to the baiting, the dreadful woman would go away.

"Lady Farren? I do not believe I have had the pleasure of making her acquaintance." Mrs. March's eyes took on a gleam of interest at the mention of a title.

The contredanse ended, and Clive and Caro returned to Julia's side. She introduced Mrs. March to her relatives. Her manner was so formal, Caro immediately surmised that the widow was not someone with which Julia wished to associate.

Although she did not give her the cut direct, Caro replied to Mrs. March in such cool tones that soon the widow all but flounced off. After that, friends on the other side of the room hailed Mrs. Crowley, giving Julia a moment's privacy with her cousin.

"What is the issue with the pretty little widow?"

Julia rolled her eyes. "Ever since I came home from

London last spring, she has not ceased prodding me about it. She just hinted that I had come to Bath to escape a scandal."

"Oh no," Caro said, a worried frown beginning to form on her brow.

Julia certainly did not want her cousin to think her enjoyment of the evening was dampened. "I do not give a fig what Widow March says. Women like her thrive on vicious gossip. Let us not give her another thought."

Caro's smile was a little uncertain as she nodded in agreement. At that moment Clive returned. By his side was a handsome gentleman who folded himself into a flourishing bow before Julia.

Julia looked from the gentleman to Clive in some surprise.

"Miss Allard, this is Mr. Dillingham, a friend of mine from school days."

"How do you do, Mr. Dillingham," Julia said as the man unfolded himself.

"Very well, Miss Allard. I understand from Lord Farren that you are from Chippenham, and shall be in Bath for some time." His intense, pale blue eyes had not left hers since he had risen from his bow.

"Your information is correct, sir."

"And are you finding Bath to your liking?"

"Indeed, I am." Julia had the distinct urge to laugh at the intensity of Mr. Dillingham's gaze, but managed to suppress everything but a smile. In truth, he was a handsome, refined-looking gentleman, and she was feminine enough to feel gratified by his regard.

"Ah, the opening strains of the Devonshire minuet," he pronounced, glancing up at the orchestra. "Miss Allard, would you do me the honor?"

His expression was so hopeful, so earnest, she would not have dreamed of declining him. "I'd be delighted, Mr. Dillingham."

As he led her to the floor, they moved past Mrs. March. Julia swiftly looked away, but not before catching the ill-tempered, narrowed-eyed look the widow gave her.

Even here in Bath, she could not escape the damage that cursed kiss had caused her, she thought with a flash of anger as she took her place next to Mr. Dillingham. Would she ever be free of that dashed duke's licentious act?

Chapter Five

That evening, the Duke of Kelbourne found himself looking down at a pair of deuces held casually in his left hand. His right hand caressed a stack of gold coins as he glanced up at his fellow gamblers lounging around the table, his expression impassive.

They were a dashed cautious lot, he mused, stifling a yawn.

In spite of his lowly deuces, he was confident that he would come out the winner of this hand, too. But this thought did not give him the usual thrill—the four other gamblers gave themselves away with various tics and quirks when they had a good hand. He had found little sport this eve.

Though his boredom grew with each hand, he did not intend to end his participation in this low-stakes game.

"Heh, heh. Let's see, my turn, gentlemen?" asked Sir Bartholomew.

Kelbourne looked over at the heavyset man and mentally sighed again. This really was becoming too easy: the *heh, hehs* were a sure indication that Sir Bartholomew had a bad hand.

Even so, Kel hoped the other gentlemen would oblige him by playing into the wee hours.

It was astonishing to him that a house as large as the one his mother and grandmother occupied could feel so confining.

Shifting, he slid lower in his chair, crossed his legs at the ankles, and continued to mull over the mess of his domestic situation. He had the time, for Sir Bartholomew would agonize for some minutes before making his play.

Kel wondered what maggot in his brain had convinced him that he should come to Bath in the first place. In spite of Emmaline's plea, he should have stayed at the Keep or gone to London.

For some reason, neither of these options had appealed to him. But a week caught in the middle of the sniping and petty bickering of his mother and grandmother was more than enough to set his nerves afray.

If his relatives' behavior was not trying enough, there was Bath itself to add to his mounting list of annoyances.

He certainly admired the aesthetics of the town. With its impressive crescents and scenic parades, Bath appeared all that was civilized and elegant. But he found it a deadly dull place for any sort of amusement. And the town was teeming with cits and doddering dowagers.

Earlier that day, when old Major Collings had timorously invited Kel to his home for a few hands of cards, the duke's boredom had lifted. Finally, a bit of action! And a perfect excuse to beg off escorting his mother and sister to the parched insipidness of the Upper Rooms.

But his evening had turned out to be more gossip than gaming.

Gad. Kel stifled a yawn and rolled his shoulder. He'd been still for so long, he was growing stiff.

His attention was caught by an odd sound emanating from the other side of the table. Glancing up, he was met with the sight of Mr. Bostock's numerous chins quivering like a pudding from his snores.

His host behaved as if this was all quite commonplace and only spared a quick glance at the clock on the mantel. "It is almost half past ten, gentlemen. Last hand?"

Kel's only show of surprise was a quickly subdued quirk of his brow. If he were in London, or anywhere else for that matter, the evening would just be in bud.

This was it. Let Maman and Grandmère cut each other to shreds with their rapier wits. He was done shielding both of them. He would have his bags packed and be on his way to Kelbourne Keep before breakfast was over. As the game concluded, Mr. Bostock awoke with a snorting start and expressed surprise that it had gotten so late.

After winning the last hand, Kel rose and made his farewells. Once Major Collings had seen him to the door with the usual pleasantries, and the groom had brought around his horse, Kel decided to take a circuitous route back to the Royal Crescent.

Setting his bay to a slow canter, he left the lane and turned onto Alfred Street. The evening air felt cool and bracing against his face. He was wide-awake and restless. The moon, which was near full and bright, gave him an idea. If he rode around town long enough, mayhap the rest of the household would be asleep when he returned. It was worth the extra distance.

He was approaching the elegant south exterior of the Upper Rooms and saw a number of carriages waiting in the forecourt. Realizing it was near eleven o'clock, he knew the assembly would have concluded, thus creating this mass exodus. In London, if he found himself forced to visit Almack's, he made it a point never to enter before five minutes to eleven.

This habit vexed Sally Jersey, who took her role as a patroness seriously. He grinned a little, recalling how she never failed to take him to task for *almost* being late. *Mayhap I shall go to London.*

As he drew even with the entrance to the Rooms, he glanced over to make sure he was in no danger of colliding with a carriage merging onto the street. Framed by a glow radiating from the room behind, he saw two women stepping from the columned entryway. One of the young ladies was much taller than the other. Instantly, his eyes were drawn to her upswept hair, which glowed pale gold in the moonlight.

Swiftly, he pulled his bay to a prancing stop. Thunderstruck, he stared as the tall young lady followed the other into the interior of a carriage.

He watched the conveyance pull forward onto the lane. It made a wide turn and rolled past him down Alfred Street.

Kel knew beyond a shadow of a doubt that he had just seen the young woman he had insulted last spring. And by her attire, he had been wrong in his assumption that she was a maid.

Pulling the reins to bring his horse's head around, he lightly spurred the animal in the direction from whence he had just come. With his boredom dissolved, he decided that Bath might afford some amusement after all.

Chapter Six

"*I* own that Mr. Dillingham is a charming man, and his countenance shows much refinement, but the tattle is that he is shockingly dipped."

Julia laughed at her cousin's warning. "I only said he was a fine dancer—I do not wish to marry him."

The two young women were strolling across the wide bowling green toward a less crowded part of Sydney Gardens. Julia, accustomed to a good amount of exercise, had welcomed her cousin's suggestion of an outing.

The day was cloudless, but a chill breeze made her glad that she had brought along her large India wrap to throw over her shoulders.

Caro looked up at her cousin, tilting her head well back due to the angle of the enormous brim of the bonnet she wore. It, like the rest of her lemon-colored ensemble, was the pinnacle of fashion. Gazing down, Julia thought Caro had an air of sophistication that was rather misleading.

"Don't you wish to be married?" Caro asked as she swung her reticule to and fro.

Taking in her cousin's avid expression, Julia shrugged lightly. "Not today."

"Oh, you are the droll one. You know what I mean. Has no young man ever touched your heart?"

As they meandered in a gradual ascent toward a little stand of trees, Julia gave this question some thought before answering. Caro had assured her earlier that they would find a most delightful cascade and vine-covered stone alcove in which to pause.

"Yes, I did have a *tendre* for a gentleman once," Julia finally responded in a matter-of-fact manner.

Surprised, Caro stopped walking to stare up at her. "You did! Who was it? What happened?"

"It was years ago," Julia replied. "I was eighteen and terribly smitten with Steven Thorncroft. I thought him the most handsome, fascinating young man in the district."

"Mariah's older brother?" Caro's tone held disbelief. "How delicious. Why did you not marry him?"

"I had the mortifying experience of overhearing him discuss me with your brother at one of the assembly balls in Chippenham."

"Roland? Heavens, Julia, do not keep me on tenterhooks."

"I was standing behind a screen near the refreshments—I cannot now recall why, probably to shamelessly eavesdrop. Anyway, Roland said, 'But you have to admit, Thorncroft, Julia is a passably pretty gel.' To which Steven replied, 'Passably pretty for such a long-shanks.' "

"Oh! You are a very good mimic, but how dreadful to have overheard that."

"Indeed. I feigned illness and was taken home."

"Dear Julia, you can tell me—is Steven Thorncroft the reason you have not married?"

At the note of deep concern in her cousin's voice, Julia tossed her head back and laughed in sheer amusement.

"Lud, no. It was not long after the ball that I realized what a dull fellow he actually is. Speaks of nothing but sheep and wool prices. I now think it was just his uniform that dazzled me."

Caro frowned. Julia's story certainly was not the tragic tale of unrequited love that she was hoping to hear.

"But still, it must have hurt to have him ridicule your height," her cousin asked, trying another gambit.

Julia waved her hand dismissively. "Not for long. Besides, I *was* a gangly girl then."

"Yes, Mama says you are a late bloomer. But there are no two arguments about it now—you have become stunningly beautiful. Just look at the way the gentlemen flocked around you last night."

"Me! You had your own full circle of admiring swains."

"I did enjoy myself last evening, but I am still angry at Clive for running off to the card room right after our only dance. And then he runs off to his mama's again today!" Caro exclaimed.

The hurt in her cousin's voice could not be mistaken. Julia admitted to herself that she had not made up her mind about Clive Farren. Granted, he had welcomed Julia with genuine solicitude. She knew he took his position in the House of Lords seriously, and loved his hounds. It had also become apparent soon after her arrival that he was tied to his mother's apron strings with a very tight knot.

They reached the little cascading spring with a picturesque ivy-covered stone alcove nearby. Amid the lush, shaded green beauty, Julia pondered her cousin's obvious unhappiness. Pulling the folds of her wrap across her shoulders, she decided against making any criticism of Clive. In years to come, if the newly wed couple resolved this problem, Caro might be hurt by Julia's critical remarks, no matter how supportive the words seemed now. But speaking up about the dowager Lady Farren was another proposition.

"Do not let his mother daunt you, Caro. Have you thought about having a private word with her? You can explain—sweetly and patiently, of course—that she is monopolizing too much of your husband's time."

"I have tried that," was her glum reply. Lowering herself to the stone bench in the alcove, Caro went on, "She complained bitterly to Clive, and he scolded me for being unkind to his mama."

"I see." *I see that Clive is more boy than man.*

Julia moved to the stone bench and brushed aside a dead leaf before sitting next to Caro. Of a sudden, a very determined expression settled on her cousin's face.

"I am thinking of starting a flirtation to make him jealous."

Julia's left brow arched in surprise at this announcement. "Do you think that is wise?"

"I don't care! He is taking me for granted after only half a year. We came to Bath only because his mama must take the waters and insists Clive escort her everywhere. What a time to be away from London! I am quite vexed that I shall miss the ball Lady Thorpe is giving in honor of Princess Charlotte's wedding next month. So why should I not start a flirtation, if it suits me?"

"When you say it that way, I understand your ire, Caro dear. But I know better than most how something completely innocent can be placed in a very bad light. You must be careful of your reputation."

"I do not believe I care. And as for *your* reputation, I still say you should have stayed in London and brazened the whole thing out. In a way, the fuss-up was rather fun and would have been more so if you had stayed. What a nine day's wonder that kiss caused! All the *ton* hunted London for you. Who was the mysterious young lady who had made Kel lose his head? It was all anyone could speak of for days! Even though his friends stated they would never forget your face, no one could find you. Mama and I were forced to laugh behind our fans on many occasions."

Appalled, Julia jumped up from the stone bench and fixed her cousin with an indignant gaze. "Good Lord! I had no idea that wretched day was discussed at such length. And why in the world do you call him 'Kel'? Never say you are acquainted with that unmitigated libertine."

"Do not be a widgeon, Julia. I am not personally acquainted with the Duke of Kelbourne. It is just that *everyone* calls him 'Kel.' Every wild thing he does is gossip fodder for the beau monde. I admit that his behavior toward you was beyond the pale, but that kind of deed is exactly why his name is on everyone's tongue."

"*Every* wild thing?"

"Yes, he's always up to something shocking. An infamous bet he made with Lord Petersham is still spoken of. They wagered five thousand pounds on which rose of a particular bush would be the first to have a bee land upon it. Despite the threat of transportation, he has been involved in several duels. There are countless stories about the Duke of Kelbourne. Even the gifts he gives his mistresses cause a commotion."

"Good heavens, what sorts of gifts?"

"I should not have told you that last bit. As a married lady I may discuss such things, but should not with you."

Rolling her eyes at her cousin's prim tone, Julia

would have none of Caro's stuffy airs. "Tosh! What sorts of gifts?"

Caro instantly gave in with a grin. "His last mistress, an opera dancer called *La Perla*, received a house and four snow-white prime bloods. When he was done with her, he gave her an enormous cache of jewels, including a ruby as large as a robin's egg. She wore the jewel in a toque and named it *L'amour de Kel*. I saw the vulgar thing myself once as she tooled her white horses through Rotten Row. It is said that she tried to bring him back to her side by threatening suicide, but he sent her a note saying he could not leave his card game."

Slightly shocked at this tale, Julia reseated herself. "I would believe any horrid thing I heard concerning him."

Caro's expression was full of sympathy. "Well, I certainly do not blame you. It was too horrid to have your Season ruined in such a scandalous way. It's no wonder you have no desire to return to London."

Julia nodded her agreement and watched the crystalline water cascading down from the stony mouth of the spring. At least she had been able to give the cur a resounding slap for his insult, she mused as she contemplated the beautiful scenery.

"You never seriously answered my question."

Julia looked over at Caro. "What question was that?"

"Don't you wish to be married?"

Julia contemplated her answer. "After a fashion, I suppose I do. I am aware that I shall be five-and-twenty this fall. While not yet a spinster, it is time to start thinking of my future. On the other hand, I do not see how my life would be improved by marriage. I have the bequest from my father, so I have no financial inducement to wed. I am not lonely—how could I be when I have my lovely family and friends? I have all my interests and pursuits in the village to occupy my time. Social standing matters naught to me. So, at this time, I give marriage little thought. I would hate to marry just for the sake of convention."

"I agree with you up to a point. However, what about love? Do not look at me that way. I own I am sometimes out of patience with my Clive, but when it is all said and done—I adore him."

"Of course you do." Julia's tone was gentle in response to her cousin's defensiveness. "I do not discount love. True love is why I will not bow down to the convention that says a woman must marry—that any husband is better than no husband. I just have not met a man who has caused any strong feelings in my heart."

"Except for Steven Thorncroft," Caro said with an impish smile.

"I have a notion that I shall regret sharing my tale with you," Julia responded with a wry smile.

"Not a bit. I am growing cold here in the shade. Shall we make our way back?"

Julia agreed, and they left the cascading spring. Glancing back, she thought it would be an enchanting place to bring a book.

The talk between the two women continued in a desultory fashion. They discussed their time at the Upper Rooms and an impending visit to Caro's mother-in-law.

People were beginning to crowd into the gardens as the fashionable hour approached. The cousins had to slow their walk considerably to weave through the throng. Just as they reached the gravel path that led to the gates of the gardens, Caro pulled up short and grabbed Julia's arm tightly.

"Bless me! Julia, come this way at once—to the pavilion." Her voice was a frantic whisper as she whipped herself, and Julia, around in a different direction.

Struck by the urgency in Caro's voice, Julia did not hesitate. With swift steps they moved past some flower beds to a graveled, open space where the orchestra played on gala nights. Caro finally looked over her shoulder and stopped.

Gathering her trailing wrap, Julia looked at her cousin askance. "Heavens, what has you looking so astounded? Did you see your mother-in-law?"

Caro shook her head and gulped a breath. "I swear I saw the Duke of Kelbourne! 'Pon my soul, I cannot imagine why *he* would be in Bath."

"The Duke of . . ." Staring at her cousin in shock, Julia gasped. "You must be mistaken, Caro. Your mind has played a trick upon you because we were just speaking of him."

"Mayhap, but we will stay here for a few moments. I shall stand in front of you, and you can hide behind my bonnet."

Julia eyed doubtfully the prodigious proportions of the yellow confection upon her cousin's head.

"I am still too tall to be completely veiled. But I believe your efforts are needless. The Duke of Kelbourne would not come to Bath—it's much too tame a place for one so dissolute."

Caro's brow furrowed in worried confusion. "I own it was only the merest glimpse, but he is a difficult man to mistake."

Julia looked over Caro's bonnet and scanned the growing clusters of people. "I see no one familiar. Come, let us not cower here," she said, drawing Caro forward.

They were almost back to the path when Julia noticed a beautiful, exquisitely garbed woman staring at her from a short distance away. Julia glanced away as she and her cousin continued to move toward the entrance. A second later, her eyes moved to the man standing next to the elegant woman. He, too, was looking directly at her. Shocked, she froze.

Caro halted next to Julia, "I told you so," she whispered.

Chapter Seven

"I must say, Kel, you are certainly being more equanimous than I had expected."

Kel sent his sister a lazy smile. "I am always equanimous, m'dear sis."

Lady Fallbrook responded with an inelegant snort as they strode through the gates of Sydney Gardens. By mutual acknowledgment, brother and sister were relieved to be away from the tension at the Royal Crescent, where they had left their mother and grandmother bickering about the upcoming musical evening they were planning.

As Kel and his sister strolled along the gravel pathway between the overflowing flower beds, they paid little attention to the stir they were creating. The rumor had been steadily spreading throughout the town for days that Kelbourne was on the scene. Now, with this very public appearance confirming the fact, the cits and the gentry alike whispered and gawked. A few young bucks even followed at a discreet distance to get a better look at the style of his boots.

Lady Fallbrook engendered her share of stares, as well. The other ladies enjoying the park sighed in envy at the exquisite details of her summer silk promenade dress of gentian blue. Her headdress, with its full plumes of ostrich feathers falling to the side of her face, was equally remarked upon. No one had seen this style before, and a number of women determined to visit their milliners as soon as possible.

The two notable figures continued along in the afternoon sunshine, acknowledging with a brief inclination of the head those who had the courage to address them.

"Seriously, Kel, I am all astonishment that you have not trotted off to London or Brighton. If I were not so concerned about Maman and Grandmère, I do not believe I would have stayed above a week. I am curious to know where you have found this sudden, and unlikely, reserve of patience."

Kel shrugged as he sidestepped a nursemaid and baby. "Truth be told, I believe Maman and Grandmère enjoy their squabbling. Why else will neither of them give up and take a separate house?"

Emmaline readjusted the angle of her sunshade and nodded in agreement with her brother's assessment. "I am sure you are right. But that still does not explain why you have stayed in Bath. Yesterday, you were on the verge of having your bags packed. Today, you seem perfectly amenable to staying here."

Kel took his time answering. *Actually, I've rarely been more bored in my life, except for a few brief moments last evening when I followed a certain carriage to Laura Place.* "Bath has certain charms that are at first not apparent. Its appeal has become more apparent to me in the last few days."

Emmaline looked skeptical at her brother's languid explanation, but did not pursue her line of questioning. She was just thankful that he had decided to stay and help her deal with their cantankerous relatives.

She bent down to admire the blooms of an unusual

species of rose. An avid gardener, she had thrown herself into this pastime not long after the death of her husband six years ago.

"I have to admit that some of the gardens here rival those in the parks of London," she told her brother upon straightening. But he was not attending her. Instead, he was staring into the distance with narrowed eyes. Half turning, Emmaline tried to see what had caught his attention.

"Emma, are you acquainted with those two ladies coming toward us?"

"I see several ladies coming toward us. Whom do you mean?"

"The tall young lady in pale green with the lady in the massive yellow bonnet."

Easily locating the women he was referring to, Emmaline watched the two figures as they abruptly stopped and hurriedly took a different direction.

"The lady in yellow is Lady Farren. We met in the Pump Room not long ago when she was with her mother-in-law and I was with Grandmère. I do not know the other. Why do you ask?"

"I wish to be made known to them," Kel told his sister decisively. "Come and make the introductions."

Wearing a startled expression, Emmaline accompanied her brother as he quickened his stride to follow Lady Farren and the mysterious beauty.

Once off the pathway, Kel lost sight of them among the hedges and trees. He slowed his pace and cursed under his breath, looking around with a frown.

Emmaline halted her progress beneath a large beech.

"Kel, what on earth are you doing? Why do you wish to meet Lady Farren?" she demanded.

The duke was about to respond to his sister's

query when he saw the ladies rounding the corner of a shrub bed some thirty yards away. "Ah, here they come. Emma, this may be a bit awkward, but I greatly desire a word with the taller young lady. If you could manage to occupy Lady Farren for a few moments, you would be doing me a great service."

Nonplussed, Emmaline could only stare at her brother in complete confusion before turning curious eyes to the rapidly approaching women.

Kel took a few steps forward and saw the Beauty and her companion halt for a moment before stepping up their pace. Because of the trees, there was nothing else for them to do but continue their approach or turn around and go in the opposite way. They continued toward him and Emmaline, he noted a moment later with satisfaction.

Hoping the Beauty's good manners would prevent her from giving him the cut direct, he sent Emmaline a significant look.

The two women were almost upon him when Emmaline stepped forward and called a cheery greeting.

"Good afternoon! It is Lady Farren, is it not? I am so pleased to meet you again after our delightful conversation in the Pump Room some days ago."

Well done, Emma, the duke thought with admiration. He could always count on his sister to be awake upon every suit.

He gazed down at the Beauty, who was looking at Lady Farren with startled eyes. It was disconcerting to find that her appearance exactly matched his memory. Her perfectly sculpted features, high cheekbones, and luminous gray eyes were surprisingly familiar considering the briefness of their only encounter. He became aware of his heart beating at a fast clip and chided himself for behaving like a schoolboy. But he had to own that it was not often that he found himself in the position of making an apology to anyone, nonetheless someone he had insulted.

"How do you do, Lady Fallbrook. I do not believe you have met my cousin, Miss Allard," Lady Farren said in a hurried, breathless voice as she sketched a quick curtsy.

As Miss Allard curtsied, she did not turn her gaze from his sister's. Were her cheeks not flushed, Kel might wonder if she remembered him at all.

"How do you do, Miss Allard. I would like to make known to you both, my brother, the Duke of Kelbourne."

Both young women curtsied, and he noted with some amusement the shallowness of Miss Allard's bob. Removing his hat, he bowed with spare, precise grace while she studiously avoided his gaze.

In a manner quite uncharacteristic of him, he hesitated in front of Miss Allard. For several months now, he had vaguely wished there were some way to apologize to this woman. Because he had not believed that he would ever see her again, the words had never fully formed in his mind. Now, with her sudden and unexpected appearance before him, he was finding it difficult to express himself.

"Lady Farren, I am wondering if you recognize the variety of rose I was just examining. It is an unusual shade of pink," Emmaline said, drawing her arm through the baroness's and gently guiding her away.

Kel saw the panicked expression on Lady Farren's face before she sent a helpless look to Miss Allard. Miss Allard's countenance was unreadable, except for her flushed cheeks.

Kel decided to plunge ahead. "Miss Allard, I believe it is my good fortune to meet you today. There is no use in pretending that I do not owe you my deepest apology."

Drawing her wrap closer around her shoulders, Miss Allard made no comment to this blunt beginning. At least she was now looking at him, he noted with some satisfaction.

Gazing into her fathomless gray eyes, a warm smile came to his lips. This particular smile usually elicited a gratifying response from ladies of all ages.

"Though it has been nigh on a year, I daresay that you have not forgotten our encounter."

One of her elegant brows arched up a fraction, but she said nothing.

"You do remember our . . . er . . . brief meeting on Bolton Street in London? I will confess that if you have put the ridiculous incident out of your mind, I would count myself fortunate." He finished with a lopsided, self-deprecating smile.

The silence stretched between them for a long, uncomfortable moment.

"I remember, Your Grace."

Standing before her on the expanse of grass, with the late afternoon sun highlighting her face, Kel was struck again by her beauty. With her statuesque figure and pale gold hair, she was an artist's fantasy of a Greek goddess. He had a talent with the paints and wondered if he could possibly do justice to her magnificence if he attempted to capture her on canvas.

Catching hold of his wayward thoughts, he continued. "I will not make excuses, nor bore you with explanations—except to say that a lark got well out of hand and I am sorry."

Her closed expression did not change. "A lark?"

Somehow, this was not working out as he had planned. Her unwavering gaze was beginning to disturb him. He tried again, spreading his hands wide. "Yes. You see, I made a vow to Dame Fortune—for reasons I won't go into—to honor her by saluting with a kiss the most beautiful woman I encountered the next day."

Gad, when said aloud it sounded dashed lame. He did not add the more damning information that he had also wagered a huge sum with his friends that he would keep his vow. At her continued stare, he felt the beginnings of a flush rising up his neck, and paused to marvel that he was still capable of such a thing.

"I'd like you to know that no insult was intended."

Her brow lifted another fraction as her blush deepened.

"I mean . . . that is to say, of course it was insulting, but I did not intend for my actions to be an insult. It's just that you were the most beautiful lady I had seen, and because of the vow . . ." His voice trailed to a stop when he saw how icy her gray gaze had become.

Now I have made a hash of it. He gritted his teeth and decided his best course of action was to retreat before he made a bigger sapskull of himself.

He bowed briefly. "No reason could excuse accosting you in such a manner, Miss Allard. I thank you for allowing me this moment to apologize."

He was relieved to see Emma and Lady Farren approaching so he could put an end to this awkward encounter. Glancing back at Miss Allard, he caught a quick flash of something he could not identify in her enigmatic expression.

Lady Farren, with a bright artificial smile affixed to her lips, moved to her cousin's side. "We must hurry, dear, if we are not to be late. How lovely to see you again, Lady Fallbrook. We bid you good day, Your Grace," she said in a rush.

Both young women gave shallow curtsies and, without waiting for Kel to give them leave, departed with rapid steps.

Kel stayed where he was, watching Miss Allard's straight back as she navigated the flower beds.

"Good Lord, Kel, what is going on? I felt like a ninny prattling on to Lady Farren when she clearly wanted to run back to Miss Allard's side."

"I had a need for a private word with Miss Allard. Thank you for keeping Lady Farren occupied for a few moments."

His sister put one hand on her hip and looked up at him. "You are not going to fob me off with that fustian. Need for a private word—ha! Until Lady Farren introduced her, I would swear you had no idea who Miss Allard was."

"I did not know her name, but I am definitely acquainted with Miss Allard."

"How do you know her?"

"It is a story that will take a few moments to tell," Kel began, taking his sister's hand and placing it in the crook of his elbow. "Shall we take in the rest of the park as I reveal my shocking tale?" he said with a languid grin.

"It would not be the first time you would shock me," was his sister's acerbic reply.

After Kel had shared the entire, embarrassing story, they stopped near a pavilion at the highest point of the gardens. Emma turned to stare at him in surprise.

"Tell me you did not actually say those things to that poor girl! You cannot possibly expect her to accept such a ham-fisted apology. Has your much vaunted adroitness completely left you?"

"Yes, I did say those things. The situation was bound to be awkward by its very nature. But all things considered, I thought it went fairly well."

Emmaline rolled her eyes. "She is obviously a properly brought-up young lady. Do you not see that suggesting she might have forgotten the kiss made it sound as if she goes around kissing so many men, your kiss could be forgotten?"

"Of course not," he stated with growing annoyance.

"And saying it was just a lark—well, that's just impertinent. And saying you did not intend to insult her? What was it, then? Oh, I see—the dashing Duke of Kelbourne was kind enough to accost her on the street and kiss her in front of all and sundry. I am surprised she did not slap you again."

Kel braced his booted foot against a low stone border of a flower bed and glowered at his sister.

"You astound me, Emma. You are twisting what occurred and placing it in the worst light. Miss Allard said very little, but I am sure she accepted my apology in the spirit in which it was given."

"Truly? Did she say she accepted your apology, such as it was?"

Kel tried to recall Miss Allard's exact words. "Well, not as such. But I put down her reaction to being caught off guard. I am sure it was a bit jarring to her sensibilities to have me suddenly appear, so to speak. I do not wonder at her somewhat cold reaction."

"Humph. Well, I have no compunction in telling you that I think you handled the whole thing quite badly. Surprising, since you have always been accounted a silk-tongued devil."

They resumed their walk, but Emmaline said nothing more after taking in the frowning, contemplative expression on her brother's face.

"Oh, Julia! You look dreadful, shall I hail a sedan chair?"

Julia only shook her head in the negative as she rushed out of the park.

Upon leaving Sydney Gardens, she entered Great

Pulteney Street, with Caro close behind. Julia cared not that it was indecorous to be seen hurrying up the street in this precipitous manner. She could not recall ever feeling so overset in the whole of her life, and only wanted to return to Caro's house as quickly as possible.

"Julia, stop! I cannot keep up with you. And if you do not tell me what transpired between you and the duke, I shall go mad." Caro did her best to catch up to Julia, but because of her cousin's longer strides, Caro had to skip to stay within a few yards.

With her hands balled into fists at her side, Julia continued to hurry up the street.

"Slow down!" Caro wailed, growing breathless.

Finally, Julia slowed to a reasonable walk, half turning to toss a glance over her shoulder. "If you had not been there to witness it, I would not believe it myself." Fury flashed in her icy gaze.

"Believe what?" Caro implored.

Julia turned full around and began to walk backward. "That . . . that hulking, insufferable, odious, foppish—he attempted to apologize to me!"

Caro's mouth fell open. "Granted, his clothes are fashionable to the last stare, but there is nothing of the fop about him—sorry, please go on," she added when Julia looked as if she might scream.

"He *smiled* and tried to charm me, and said it was a *lark* that got out of hand. He even wondered if I had forgotten the whole ridiculous scene. As if I could ever forget! He did not *intend* to insult me, he said so sincerely. As if I should take it as a compliment that he decided to kiss me without my consent?" Julia threw her hands up in frustration.

Caro was silent as she waited for a Bath chair carrying an elderly woman to pass by. Julia turned back around and quickened her steps again.

"But he did apologize," Caro pointed out to her cousin's back.

"For what!" Julia almost shouted over her shoulder. "He does not even know the damage he caused me. He only bothered to approach me to assuage his own underdeveloped conscience. I've seen better acts of contrition from someone who inadvertently jostled me at an assembly ball."

Caro cringed a little at the contempt and anger in her cousin's voice.

When they reached the steps of the townhouse, Julia stopped. With her eyes flashing silver fire and her breaths coming in rapid succession, she turned to Caro. "You have no idea how much I would dearly love to repay that arrogant brute for his *lark.*"

Chapter Eight

•

*K*el was seated in the sunny morning room gazing out of the window that overlooked the expansive, sloping lawn and the lower town beyond. After several moments of fruitless reverie, he turned to the newspaper he had tossed aside earlier.

He had less luck diverting himself with the news, and with a disgusted gesture, he tossed the paper to a side table.

As he ran his long fingers through his hair, a vision of Miss Allard came immediately to mind. Her beautiful face framed by the backdrop of greenery entered his thoughts more often than he cared to admit. It was the damnedest thing. He really ought to have felt better since he'd made his apology to her. He'd always heard that getting something one felt guilty about off one's chest was a cleansing experience—or some such rot. But for some inexplicable reason, he felt worse.

He frowned as he relived the awkward scene in Sydney Gardens several days ago. Maybe it was because he had not been able to read her expression, or to gauge what she was thinking. Usually, the emotions of the female sex were transparent to him. But that was not the case with the enigmatic Miss Allard, and he found it quite disconcerting.

Mentally shrugging, he decided that as embarrassing as it had been to apologize to her, it had been the gentlemanly thing to do. With his frown deepening, he contemplated this last thought. Could that be the reason for his irritable mood? He could not recall embarrassing himself in front of any woman before—and it definitely had been embarrassing to confess his ridiculous reason for accosting her.

He found that he actually dreaded another encounter with those unflinching, unreadable gray eyes. *Wouldn't Emma get a laugh out of that?* he thought in self-disgust.

His grandmother swept into the room, saving him from any further, uncomfortable rumination.

"Ah, Wenlock," she said in her clear, well-modulated voice. "I am looking for my sunshade. Have you seen it in here?"

Rising to his feet, he glanced around the room. His grandmother was the only person who called him by the family name instead of his given name, title, or the shortened "Kel."

"No, I do not believe so, Grandmère. You are going out?" he asked, noting her fashionable bonnet and reticule. "It is almost time for tea, is it not?" He pulled his watch fob from the pocket of his deep blue waistcoat.

"Ha! Yes, it is time for tea, and yes, I am going out." She looked up at him with hazel eyes very like his own and gave her kid glove a good tug, then straightened the collar of her russet-and-cream pelisse.

Knowing that sharp tone was invariably connected to his mother, Kel did not ask any more questions, hoping to escape before she went into a full-blown diatribe. By the look of her compressed lips and pinched nostrils, she was not far from exploding.

"Your flibbertigibbet mother is having tea with her flibbertigibbet friends. I shall have tea elsewhere—if I can locate that annoying sunshade. I do not know how an object that size can be continually misplaced."

Kel again made a show of looking around the room for the elusive sunshade. For as long as he could remember, this had been the constant theme between his mother and grandmother. His grandmother took offense if she was not always treated with the respect she believed was her due. Maman, on the other hand, saw no need to defer to her mother-in-law on any matter.

Still, he was a little surprised that Grandmère, with her surfeit of pride and sense of her own consequence, would leave the house instead of holding court here.

The old lady was still complaining about the missing sunshade when her flustered maid hurried into the room, holding the desired article aloft. "I found it, Your Grace!" she exclaimed before dropping a curtsy.

"So you have. Where on earth was it hiding?"

"In the breakfast room, ma'am."

"Of course, logical place for it," the dowager muttered sourly.

Kel smiled at her grousing, but remained silent. Tightening the bow of her stylish bonnet, Alice, the dowager Duchess of Kelbourne, eyed her grandson with keen interest.

"I must say, I never expected you to last this long. Thought you'd have raced off to London days ago."

"I am finding my stay restful."

His pronounced urbanity caused her to guffaw.

"Looks like you're suffering from the blue-devils if you ask me. Care to escort me on my little excursion? It's a fine day for a walk."

"My apologies, but no, thank you, Grandmère. I desire to lounge this afternoon." No offense to his grandmother, but if he was bored now, he could not imagine what he would be feeling if he spent the afternoon with her and her cronies.

With a little shrug, the dowager crossed to the doorway. "You shall suit yourself as usual." Once in the hall, he heard her call to her maid and footman. "Come, Philips, come, Henry—we cannot keep Lady Farren waiting."

Long strides carried Kel to the hallway, where he caught up to his grandmother.

"Grandmère, I believe I will join you after all. I shall fetch my hat and be with you in a moment."

Pausing, his grandmother looked up at him with surprise evident on her thin features. "Certainly, Wenlock, but do hurry."

A lackey was dispatched to get his hat and silver-tipped walking stick. As they waited, Kel was keenly aware of his grandmother's discerning gaze upon him.

The moment they left the house, with the maid and footman following behind, the dowager duchess launched into a list of grievances against Kel's mother.

"Really, Wenlock, the people your mother allows into my house! Witless ninnies and mincing fops." She tapped her sunshade on the cobbles for emphasis.

"There is a remedy, you know," was his dry reply.

"Yes! Millicent can leave. Why should I bestir myself from that perfectly charming house? I invited her to stay as my guest—if she does not like how I run my household, she can just take herself off."

Shrugging his shoulders in a noncommittal fashion, Kel thought again that this situation was the reason why he had kept a bachelor household for the last ten years. As much as he loved his mother and grandmother, holidays and the occasional visits were more than enough.

"I shall speak to Maman. It should take very little effort to convince her to take another house."

The dowager stopped dead still on the sidewalk and looked up at her grandson. "Don't you dare! I would not have Millicent think I have run to you with complaints."

Adjusting the angle of his hat, Kel looked heaven-ward for patience.

"Perhaps if you would try to see it from Maman's perspective, this situation might be more tenable. And I shall speak to her about being more reason-able also."

"Her perspective! Be more reasonable! Why, you wound me—I am the most reasonable person I know."

Kel chuckled. "Come, now, Grandmère, it is too fine a day to squabble, and we don't often have the chance to take a walk together."

"You are right, let us move to more pleasant subjects."

"How are you acquainted with Lady Farren?" Kel asked in a deceptively offhand manner.

"Deirdre? Known her for years. One of the most annoying creatures who ever lived. Talks of nothing but that milk-and-water son of hers. But for all that, she can be rather amusing."

Kel's pleasure in the outing suddenly dissipated. "I take it we are calling on the *dowager* Lady Farren?"

"Of course. I certainly would not call upon her daughter-in-law, though I would be at home to her if she called upon me."

Kel sighed. Deeply.

They arrived at the house some minutes later. The

butler led them to a drawing room crowded with overly ornate furniture. Kel immediately took in the others who were seated in the congested room.

A plump, older woman with a profuse amount of unlikely guinea gold hair was obviously the dowager baroness. He recognized Lady Farren and surmised that the blond man seated next to her was her husband. Finally, Kel's gaze moved to the other occupant of the room.

A lazy smile spread across his features as his eyes briefly met a pair of icy gray eyes. "Good afternoon, Miss Allard."

Julia's shock at seeing the duke again was almost as great as it had been at Sydney Gardens. As the butler announced the new guests, she flashed one look to the duke's tall figure filling the doorway, and then threw a stunned glance to Caro.

At the duke's greeting, Julia's voice seemed stuck in her throat. "Good afternoon, Your Grace," she managed to choke out.

After that, the rest of the introductions were a bit of a blur, but Julia had the impression that the distinguished-looking older woman on the duke's arm was his grandmother.

Once everyone was seated, and the tea poured and passed, Julia knew she must catch hold of her escalating panic.

For a split second, when he had first walked into the room, she thought she might lose control. She did not know if she wanted to slap him again, or run out of the room. Having grown accustomed to thinking of him as her most hated enemy, it was now difficult to behave as if everything were perfectly normal.

But what else could she do? Causing a scene would not accomplish her desire of exacting some kind of revenge, and would only reflect badly on Caro.

Without calling attention to herself, she slowly set her teacup on the little rosewood table next to her chair. She did not trust her still shaking fingers not to make a clatter. Linking her hands together, she placed them in her lap, and forced her features into what she hoped was a serene expression.

Why had she not taken the opportunity to tell him exactly what she thought of him when they were at Sydney Gardens?

It vexed her no end that when she finally had the chance to vent a year's worth of suppressed anger, she had let the opportunity slip through her fingers. Granted, she had been so astonished by his sudden appearance that she had little chance to formulate her thoughts, much less marshal a proper tirade.

Now it seemed that it was too late to rage at him.

She watched him as he conversed with the others in his smooth manner. It seemed to her that the duke, with his air of cool sophistication, did not fit into this cozy scene. She almost rolled her eyes in disgust at the way Lord Farren and his mother fawned and gushed over the duke, who behaved as if it were his due.

Pulling her gaze from him, Julia glanced at his grandmother with curiosity. It was difficult to imagine that a man as vile as the Duke of Kelbourne actually had something as mundane as a grandmother.

The dowager duchess was a formidable-looking woman, with thin, sharp features, whose straight posture and slim figure belied her age. And despite her advanced years, her ensemble was extremely fashionable, but with no hint of mutton dressed as lamb. Julia admired the fineness of the lace at the elegant lady's neck, and thought the older woman's appearance was in flattering contrast to the dowager Lady Farren's overly fussy and girlish attire.

"Miss Allard, how are you enjoying your stay in Bath?"

It took Julia a moment to respond, she was so taken aback by the dowager duchess's question. "Very well, Your Grace."

"You do not find it dull? I would think a pretty gel like you would be in London this time of year."

Julia exchanged a swift, speaking glance with Caro. She wondered how the duke's grandmother would react if she informed the imperious-looking duchess exactly why she was not in London. "I prefer to visit with my cousin, Your Grace."

The dowager Lady Farren recalled the duchess's attention, and for once, Julia was grateful for the lady's incessant chatter.

Feeling the duke's gaze upon her, Julia could not prevent herself from glancing in his direction. The expression on his rugged-angled features and in his eyes could only be described as questioning. Giving no sign of noticing, she turned to attend the general conversation.

"And how do you know our Miss Allard?" the dowager Lady Farren asked the duke.

"We were introduced in Sydney Gardens a few days ago," he replied, sending Julia an almost conspiratorial smile.

Julia looked away and busied herself with her teacup. How dare he grin at her with such odious condescension! Fervently, she prayed that this second disturbing encounter with the duke would end before she lost control of the anger seething beneath her cool demeanor.

His answer seemed to satisfy Caro's mother-in-law, and the general conversation continued. But soon,

Julia became aware of the dowager duchess's frank gaze frequently upon her. In growing nervousness, she wondered what the duchess could be about.

"Miss Allard, I would like to compliment you on your excellent posture."

Relieved that the duchess had not broached anything more personal, Julia's smile was natural for the first time since the lady and her grandson had entered the room.

"I thank you, ma'am."

The dowager nodded approvingly. "Most tall young ladies slouch about, thinking to disguise their height, when it does nothing of the sort. Wenlock, do not you agree with me?"

Her grandson turned from his conversation with Lord Farren and smiled engagingly.

"With what, Grandmère? That Miss Allard has elegant posture? Or slouching does not hide one's height?"

"Oh, you!" She tapped his knee before addressing the rest of them in tones of obvious affection for her grandson. "Wenlock has always been a great one for teasing and pranks. Forever full of high spirits."

Oh, indeed, Julia thought before casting the duke a look of such complete condemnation that it caught his attention.

"Teasing and pranks can often misfire." The look he gave Julia as he said this was so pointed that she caught her breath in mortification.

Shooting a nervous glance to the duchess and Lady Farren, she prayed that they would not think anything strange about the duke's remark.

"You are so right, Your Grace," Caro put in quickly. "My older brother, Roland, was a dreadful prankster when we were children. I used to get so angry at him I would chase him with our papa's crop. Thank heavens he has outgrown such nonsense and is now very nice."

To Julia's immense relief, the duke's remark passed without further comment, although Lord Farren did appear amused at his wife's uncharacteristic babbling.

Furtively casting the duke a quick glance, Julia saw that he was still gazing at her with an assessing expression. Quickly turning away, Julia lifted her chin and determined to ignore him until this wretched tea concluded.

Chapter Nine

Several nights later, Julia found herself in the midst of a ball taking place in the dowager Lady Farren's grand house. And it was apparent to all that the bejeweled dowager had spared no expense to impress Bath society.

By London standards, it was not a large affair, but the dowager was pleased to the point of simpering with the number of illustrious personages now dancing in her salon. The room was normally used for card parties and large dinners, but with the furniture and the rugs removed, it served well as a ballroom.

Standing near the large fireplace, its grate aglow with flowers instead of flames, Julia could not help admiring the beautiful room. The dowager certainly had excellent taste. The light from hundreds of candles in the crystal chandelier cast a warm glow across the polished floors. There were numerous tall, free-standing candelabra in the corners of the room, with garlands of ivy, lilies, and tuberoses twining up the stands and secured by yards of gold ribbon.

Inhaling the subtly sweet fragrance of the blooms in the hearth, Julia realized she was having a wonderful time. The excellent orchestra was currently playing a cotillion, and the lilting notes were in perfect harmony with the heady scent of the flowers and the swaying, vibrant silks of the ladies' gowns.

She had been discreetly admiring several pairs of dancers throughout the evening. One pair in particular, an older couple, were obviously and unashamedly besotted with each other. The way they gazed into each other's eyes during the allemande reminded her of her aunt and uncle. Several other couples of varying ages displayed the same charming behavior.

With an appreciative smile playing on her lips, she watched these couples and began to wonder. How did one go about finding a true love? Having never met a man who caused any sort of heightened emotion within her—she dismissed her brief, youthful fancy of Steven Thorncroft—she wondered how it was done.

A few years ago, she had raised the subject with Aunt Beryl and Uncle John, and the consensus seemed to be that one just knew when one met their true love. Her aunt had described in great detail the flutters she had experienced when she first laid eyes upon her beloved John.

Was that it? Did one just hope to chance upon the right person? And when one did, was there some sort of telltale vapors or palpitations?

While growing up, she had also heard that some women were not meant to fall in love. Could she be one of those? It was a disturbing thought. After all, she was four and twenty, and it seemed that if someone were going to engage her heart, it would have happened by now.

Her eyes sought out Mr. Dillingham. He was partnering Lady Drake, and Julia followed his elegant movements for some moments. He was certainly a handsome man—and his manners were exceptional— but nothing about him caused any kind of breathlessness or heart fluttering.

Just then, Caro moved to Julia's side, interrupting her ponderings. "I have spoken little to you this evening, dear cousin. Let us take a turn around the room and see if we can find a private spot."

Smiling down, Julia set aside her musings to attend her cousin.

Soon they found a corner where they were partially shielded by a voluminous potted fern balanced on a Corinthian-style pedestal.

"Oh, my dear, you must be fatigued after all the dancing you have done," Caro said.

"Indeed. I'm glad we found this quiet place before Mr. Gordon can beseech me to dance again," Julia said, laughing lightly.

"How delicately put! What you really mean to say is you are glad you got away before Mr. Gordon attempts to tread on your toes again."

"I confess you are right, and my shoes bear the evidence." She grimaced as she raised the hem of her gown an inch or two to reveal the smudges on her pale blue dancing slippers.

"At least there is Mr. Dillingham to dance with. The two of you are very graceful together."

"Thank you. He is a very accomplished dancer. Mr. Gordon aside, I am having a lovely time."

Caro sighed and peeped around the fern before replying to her cousin. "It is a lovely evening—I will give my mother-in-law that much credit."

"As much as it pains you to say so," Julia said with gentle humor.

The younger woman made a face in response. Julia thought the pouting expression was in stark contrast with the sophisticated façade Caro usually presented.

Adjusting her oyster-shell silk shawl, Caroline sniffed. "Well, I certainly am not so churlish that I will not give credit where it is due."

Julia glanced through the gauzy leaves of the fern, her eyes chancing upon the dowager Lady Farren holding court on the other side of the room.

Julia had noticed before that the dowager liked to think of herself as up to every rig and went to great pains to be considered in the latest mode. But Julia thought the multitude of peacock feathers erupting from the bright green turban the lady wore looked quite comical.

Since the start of the evening, she had also noticed that whenever her son strayed too far from her side, his mama called him back on the pretext of needing his opinion or some other transparent nonsense.

Caro had been subtly punishing her husband by staying as far from the dowager as possible, thereby forcing Lord Farren to trot from one end of the salon to the other whenever his mama beckoned him from his wife's side.

It would all have been rather amusing if Julia were not completely aware of how upset Caro really was.

Lord Farren, poor fellow, seemed flustered. When he was at his mama's side, he could barely take his eyes from his wife, and frowned fiercely as she laughed with her circle of friends.

Conversely, when he was with Caro, he continually glanced nervously in his mother's direction.

Julia almost felt sorry for him.

"I half expected to see the Duke of Kelbourne tonight," Caro stated.

"Good gracious! Why ruin a perfectly wonderful evening by mentioning that man? I am prodigiously pleased that I have not laid eyes upon him since tea here. I hope he has taken himself off to London—or anywhere else, for that matter."

"It's possible. But I know my mother-in-law invited the Kelbournes."

" 'Tis almost midnight, so I believe we have been spared his detestable company," Julia stated with satisfaction.

"I confess I found his grandmother quite daunting, but his sister was charming. The duke certainly seems to treat them with great solicitude."

Julia gave a little shrug in response. Truth be told, as much as she loved her cousin, Julia was hurt by her couched defense of the duke. After all, Caro knew better than anyone what the duke's so-called lark cost her. It was above annoying to see how she followed her husband and mother-in-law in gushing over the duke—albeit not as obviously.

"When I think of how he smirked at me during tea, I still seethe. He must have won a large wager to still gloat over that kiss—such arrogant condescension is not to be born."

Tilting her head to the side, Caro hesitantly cleared her throat.

"You have enough reason to dislike the duke, Julia, but I did not think he smirked at you. I thought he was trying to give you a reassuring smile. As if to let you know that he would never bring up the circumstances of your first meeting."

Julia gazed at her cousin in hurt surprise. "I own I am very sensitive regarding the duke. But have you forgotten what happened last year? To this day, people in my village think that I must have done something scandalous to be sent home from London. I never attended a ball, or the theater. You said yourself that I was the subject of gossip after I left. Good heavens, men made wagers about me!"

The expression on her cousin's face changed completely as Caro reached over and gripped her arm. "Julia, I am horrible! I have forgotten how awful it must have been for you! Forgive me, I have been insensitive and churlish. It is just so easy to be lulled by his charm. Don't you think he is terribly dashing?"

"Not in the least—but let us not waste one more moment discussing him. I shall hate him even more if he causes any awkwardness between us."

"Oh, my dear, that can never happen." Caro gave Julia's arm an affectionate squeeze.

In companionable silence, they watched the other guests from the relative privacy behind the pedestal. Dismissing thoughts of the hated duke, Julia took a moment to ponder the letter she had received earlier that day from Mariah Thorncroft. The missive had stated that Mariah and her mother would be coming to Bath in the next day or two.

Before receiving this news, Julia had almost decided to return home, despite Caro's protests, but now she knew she must stay for Mariah's sake. Besides, she had not seen the duke for days. Hopefully, the rest of her stay in Bath would be peaceful.

Catching sight of Lord Farren looking around the room, Julia turned to Caro. "I believe your husband is seeking your company."

Caro sniffed. "Ah, his mama must be quite diverted to let him get away."

"Oh, Caro, I hate to see you so upset."

"Not to worry, I am not as upset as I seem to be. I have come to realize that Clive will eventually have to choose his mother or me. It is that simple. I have ceased to harangue him or pout. When he runs off to her side, I endeavor to enjoy myself anyway."

"I believe you are wise in this plan. His attention seems to be on you even when he is at his mama's side," Julia said, trying to be encouraging.

Caro's face brightened. "Oh, do you think so?" she questioned, peeping around the fern.

As they stepped out from their hiding place, Julia put her arm through Caro's and drew her back to the main part of the room.

When Lord Farren saw them, he smiled and hurried forward. "There you are, Caro. Julia, I know you will forgive me if I take your cousin from you. My mother has given permission for a waltz to be played, and I wish to claim my wife's hand."

Caro beamed up at her husband, and Julia again thought that Caro was showing great wisdom in her handling of this difficult situation.

With deliberate ceremony, Lord Farren led his beautiful wife to the floor. Julia noticed that there were only four other couples with the pluck to join Lord and Lady Farren in performing the daring dance.

Glancing around at the other guests watching from the edges of the floor, Julia noticed the number of older people looking on disapprovingly.

Lud, Bath really could be stuffy. At the assembly balls back home, couples waltzed with nary an eyebrow raised by even the most straitlaced. Undaunted, Caro and Clive took their places as the lilting strains of the waltz began.

A smile came to Julia's lips when she saw the older couple she had been admiring all evening performing the steps with smooth grace.

"What a lovely sight you present, Miss Allard, framed by the flowers and candles—like a goddess in her bower."

Julia turned to see Mr. Dillingham standing next to her. Admiring his attractive dimples, she paused to assess her heartbeat, just in case. It would have been nice to fall in love with so amiable a man.

"You catch me at a loss for words, Mr. Dillingham—so I shall only say thank you for your kind flattery."

Placing a hand over his heart, Mr. Dillingham gave her a mock look of pain. "You wound me, Miss Allard, my words are a true expression of my feelings! And you call it mere flattery—I thought it was closer to poetry."

"I sincerely apologize, sir, for not properly appreciating your poetry," she said with a twinkle in her eyes.

The smile on Mr. Dillingham's face stilled as his eyes swept over her features.

"You really are the loveliest young lady I have ever seen."

Julia suddenly felt shy at the serious tone in his soft voice, and was at a loss as to how to reply.

As if he sensed the change in her mood, his voice changed back to a lighter tone as he asked her if she waltzed.

"Yes, I do."

"Mayhap in the future you will honor me with a waltz."

Julia smiled but made no response and continued to watch the dancers.

Though Mr. Dillingham stayed by her side, he said little else.

This was a familiar scene, Julia thought with a mental sigh. Here they were at the beginning of a perfectly fine conversation, and he had to go and make it awkward by becoming too serious. Why did gentlemen do that? Continuing their banter would have been much more fun. She hoped he was not developing a *tendre* for her. It would be too bad to have to start avoiding him—he was such a good dancer.

At that moment their hostess approached, and Julia thought her green turban and tight aubergine-colored gown made her look rather like an eggplant.

"La, Miss Allard, does not my son dance beautifully?" Her high, breathless voice seemed at odds with her plump, matronly figure.

"Indeed he does, my lady."

"Yes, he takes after me. I would have thought that he would partner me for the first waltz—he is usually the most considerate son."

Out of sheer loyalty to Caro, Julia could not let this pass and looked down at the matron with a raised brow. "Well, my lady, I think it is most appropriate for Lord Farren to waltz with his new wife," she stated, trying to keep the edge of anger from her voice.

The lady's mouth dropped open in surprise, and she sputtered in her attempt to respond.

Julia tensed, ready to continue her defense of Caro. Suddenly the dowager's mouth closed, and her eyes lit up as she espied something over Julia's shoulder.

"Bless me! The Duke of Kelbourne has decided to grace my little ball!"

Julia's heart sank to her slippers as she whipped her head around to see the duke. He was standing in the frame of the open double doors, gazing around the room with that bored yet somehow assessing expression.

At his right was his sister, her gleaming golden gown showing to great advantage against her brother's black coat.

The waltz was ending, and Julia watched as Lady Farren hurried across the floor, waving her handkerchief at the newcomers.

Caro and Clive left the floor and came to join Julia and Mr. Dillingham. There was no mistaking the concern in Caro's eyes as they met Julia's startled gray gaze.

"Well, we are certainly in rare company," Mr. Dillingham said, his eyes on the duke.

"Yes, we are certainly honored to have the duke

and Lady Fallbrook at our ball—though it is a bit late," Clive added.

"Not in London," Caro could not resist pointing out. "When we were in Town, the best parties seldom started before midnight."

They watched as Clive's mother presented a few people to the duke and his sister. A moment later Mr. Dillingham bowed and took himself off.

"Oh, Julia, are you all right?" Caro asked as soon as Mr. Dillingham was out of earshot.

Clive leaned his slim frame forward to look at Julia with concern. "Why should she not be?"

"Never mind, Clive. Julia?"

"I am perfectly well. I am sure Lady Farren wishes you to make welcome her new guests. I shall be fine here." She forced her voice to a lightness she did not feel.

Caro looked back with obvious concern as her husband drew her away.

Lifting the hem of her lavender-blue gown, Julia moved through the other guests to a less conspicuous part of the room. Keeping her eye on the duke was easy; he was at least a head taller than any other man present. Her eyes slightly narrowed, she followed the duke's broad-shouldered frame as he made his way across the room.

Turning her head slightly, Julia watched a smiling Mr. Dillingham approach Lady Fallbrook. After a moment Julia's eyes moved back to the duke, who was now conversing with an older gentleman.

She had to own that though he was not handsome in the traditional sense, he was striking. She could acknowledge this without diluting her hatred of him. Inexplicably, the fact that he was so attractive made her loathing that much more intense.

For what seemed like the thousandth time, she wished that there were a way she could make him pay for that kiss. His *lark,* she seethed. She wanted him to know what he had done to her, the trouble he had caused her. But how? Her brow creased in contemplation. He was a powerful man; there was nothing someone like her could do to wipe that arrogant look off his face. How could he, who cared not that the world knew him to be an unmitigated rakehell, understand what it was like for a woman to be at risk of losing her good name—through no fault of her own.

Nothing could hurt a man like him, she thought, gripping her fan in impotent rage.

Her anger simmering, she watched him for a few minutes longer. As his teeth flashed in laughter at something the older gentleman said, her heart jumped at a sudden thought.

Gripping her sandalwood fan tighter, she allowed the unprecedented, extraordinary thought to stay a moment.

The notion was so daring, so out of character, that she tried to dismiss it.

Flipping open her fan, she used it vigorously to cool her flushed cheeks. Her angry, troubled eyes returned to the duke. The extraordinary idea would not leave.

A thrill of daring and danger raced across her body, raising gooseflesh down her spine. She tried to consider the ramifications of carrying out this hazy and hurriedly designed plan.

Without vanity, she knew most people of her acquaintance considered her pretty. By the very fact that the duke had used her to keep his ridiculous vow, he must have thought so, too.

With her heart racing and the heady scent of the flowers and candles assailing her overwrought senses, Julia came to a decision.

Maybe, just maybe, if she were bold enough and

applied some of Caro's advice on flirting—and if there were any fairness at all in the world—she could pull it off.

Lifting her chin, she stepped away from the wall and began to move slowly toward Caro's mother-in-law. As if her hazardous decision had somehow heightened her senses, she was aware the instant the duke's eyes found her.

Could she really do it? She experienced a moment of hesitation, as if she were about to walk into a darkened room with no idea what lay ahead.

Pushing aside the specter of fear and throwing away all caution, she turned fully around and looked directly at the duke. Above the heads of the swaying dancers, she allowed a slow and, she hoped, alluring smile to spread across her lips.

Chapter Ten

There was nothing hesitant or shy about the way his gaze met and stayed on hers. Breathless at the shock his intense, glittering gaze caused her senses, Julia realized nothing in her life had prepared her for a moment like this.

Trying to calm her galloping pulse, she forced herself to breathe slowly—it would be mortifying to have him know how nervous she was. There was something so knowing, so assessing in his gaze, that she found it more difficult than she had imagined to hold his gaze.

From the corner of her eye, Julia saw the petite figure of Mrs. Crowley approaching. Unhurriedly, she pulled her gaze from the duke's, but not before she saw a rakish half-smile appear on his lips.

Turning, she smiled her response to Mrs. Crowley's greeting. So tightly strung were her senses, she was almost physically attuned to the moment the duke moved.

Without looking in his direction, she was aware of his tall frame strolling around the edge of the dance floor, stopping here and there to speak with other guests.

"Do you not think the waltz is lovely?"

Pulling her attention back to Mrs. Crowley, Julia quickly nodded, lest the lady think she was rude. "Yes, and terribly romantic."

"Only a few of the grand hostesses here in Bath allow the waltz to be danced at their private gatherings. The Master of Ceremonies at the Upper Room will not hear of allowing the waltz," the older lady stated, before turning her attention back to the dancers.

Julia turned her attention to the floor also, and her gaze swept the festive, colorful crowd. For the first time, she noticed a large gilt-framed pier glass hanging on the opposite wall.

Because she was at a slight angle, she could see a good part of the room, and was able to admire the swaying gowns and glittering jewels reflected in the glass.

A moment later, she caught sight of the duke and discreetly kept her eyes upon his reflection.

She hated his arrogant, handsome face with every fiber of her being. Watching how everyone feted and gushed over him steeled her resolve to exact some kind of revenge—to pierce his pride in the only way she knew how. The graceful music and the happy hum of the guests only seemed to accentuate the power of her feelings.

She continued to watch the pier glass as he made his way inexorably closer to her. With every step he took, her heart beat a little faster and her breath seemed to pause tremulously in her throat.

Mrs. Crowley stayed at her side, chatting about the dancers. Julia was grateful not to be alone at this moment.

The duke disengaged himself from a gentleman, and as he turned away, their gazes met in the pier glass. Her eyes froze on his, and she was astonished that the unexpected meeting felt almost like a physical touch.

Instinctively, she glanced away. But a moment later, she stiffened her resolve and turned her gaze back to his.

He was much closer to her now, and she felt the gooseflesh rise down the length of her arms. This was the moment, she thought in rising waves of panic. And she knew, with a conviction as clear as the music that filled the room, that her entire plan hinged on this moment.

"Good evening, Miss Allard."

Had she noticed how deep his voice was before this moment, she wondered as the deep timbre vibrated over her skin.

Lifting her chin slightly, she looked directly into his disturbing hazel eyes.

"Good evening, Your Grace, are you acquainted with Mrs. Crowley?" she asked, curtsying before turning to present the petite matron.

Mrs. Crowley flushed and choked on a giggle and actually curtsied twice.

With smooth, spare grace, the duke inclined his head to Mrs. Crowley.

"Oh, Your Grace, we are so pleased to have you in Bath," Mrs. Crowley gushed.

The duke raised one brow and flicked a quick amused glance to Julia, and she felt slightly taken aback by the intimate, conspiratorial feeling that look evoked within her.

As he responded to Mrs. Crowley, Julia was aware of what a novel experience it was for her to be next to a man so much taller than she was. It was something she rarely encountered, and it was not just his height but the imposing breadth of his shoulders that made her feel almost petite for the first time in her life.

The melody of the waltz faded away, and Julia saw Caro leading Clive over, her expression anxious.

The orchestra struck up the opening notes of a quadrille.

Again, a thrill raced up Julia's spine at her daring. She knew that any second Caro would try to rescue her. She must act quickly if she were to seize this chance. With a confidence born of a year's worth of suppressed anger, she gave the duke an intimate look of her own.

Julia held her breath and waited. She hoped fervently that he would unwittingly aid her in her plan to exact her revenge upon him.

"Miss Allard, if you are spoken for this set, I shall be desolate," he drawled with an answering smile.

"No, this dance is not bespoken, Your Grace."

"Would you do me the honor?"

With a gesture of supreme confidence, he held out his hand toward her. Lifting her hand toward his, his long fingers engulfed hers. The moment she felt the warmth of his fingers through her glove, that same breathless feeling came over her once again.

Looking down at her slim hand held by his strong fingers, she paused for a moment before moving off with him.

The other dancers took their places, and Julia was keenly aware that a number of eyes were directed toward her and the duke.

Keeping her expression as composed as she could, she glanced over and saw Caro standing next to Clive with her mouth agape. Julia had to look away from the stunned expression on her cousin's face, for she was afraid she would lose her nerve.

As the music rose, Julia abandoned herself to the mood permeating the flower-scented, candlelit room. Purposely and with determination, she set aside any trepidation that still lingered.

The dance began with them facing each other, followed by several turns and passes.

At the first pass, in the chassé style, she took her courage in both hands, and with a little toss of her head, she gave the duke her most dazzling smile and passed him much too closely, her bare shoulder lightly brushing the sleeve of his black evening coat.

As she did this, she looked up at him and felt a little disheartened when he did not react as she hoped. Not that she was at all sure what to expect—certainly not the slightly amused quirk of a smile he shot her. But at least he made no evasive move.

Through the steps of the dance, they came together and parted numerous times, saying nothing. He was a very good dancer, she observed, continuing to move as close to him as possible, gazing into his eyes in what she hoped was a fascinating manner.

With a feeling of deflation, she noticed he did not appear to be at all dazzled. She guessed that was too much to hope for in a matter of five minutes—especially from a jaded rake.

But he was gazing at her with a disturbing intensity, curiously in contrast with the sophisticated, enigmatic smile he wore. During the exchange where the gentlemen circled the ladies, he took her lead and moved behind her, so near that she felt his warmth on the back her bare nape.

Suppressing a shiver of awareness, she glanced over her shoulder to gaze at him with an expression of open admiration.

Never in the whole of her life had she behaved in such a forward manner. In the part of her mind that could still think clearly, she knew that if they were here, her aunt and uncle would be looking at her disapprovingly.

They met in the center, held hands, and crossed in front of each other; she moved so closely in front of him that she saw the green flecks surrounding the inky pupils of his chestnut eyes.

Something about his unaffected self-confidence rattled her sense of purpose. It occurred to her that it would be much easier to carry out her scheme if he were not so terribly attractive. And it was more than galling to realize that he found it perfectly natural *for her to be* flirting with him in this unguarded way. Oh, she wanted to see that arrogant expression wiped off his face.

She gave him another sideways little smile, allowing her gaze to linger on his for several seconds too long. As hard as she tried, she could not hold his piercing gaze and was the first to look away.

Another moment of heart-thumping panic gripped her. How could she do this? The wisest thing she could do was stop this nonsense before it went further. It was certainly not too late to extricate herself from what at this stage could only be termed as a mild flirtation.

But another glance at his arrogant countenance kept her from retreating.

Resolutely, she pushed thoughts of tomorrow from her mind. There was only tonight and the disturbing presence of her hated enemy. If she could secure his interest now, she would decide what to do about it later.

Making another graceful turn, she realized it would be easier said than done.

Glancing around, she saw that more than a few pairs of eyes were upon her and the duke as they went through the steps of the dance. The staid residents of Bath were certainly being treated to a rare sight this evening.

A devilish smile lurked at the corner of his mouth as they met in the center, hands clasping briefly before separating again. Schooling her breathing to a slower pace, she sent him a smile that she hoped conveyed that she welcomed his touch.

Finally, to her great relief, the quadrille ended and the duke was unhurriedly guiding her back to where Caro was standing, staring at her in near horror.

The pounding of Julia's heart had nothing to do with dancing as the duke amiably greeted Lord and Lady Farren.

She held her breath, hoping he would not just bow and take his leave.

Caro was still gazing at Julia, but her expression was not as obviously appalled as it had been a few moments ago. It was apparent that she was making an effort to regain her composure.

Knowing from past experience that sometimes Caro spoke before thinking, Julia hoped her cousin would not blurt out something foolish.

Before anything other than pleasantries could be exchanged, Clive's mama called to him. Bowing to Julia and the duke, he took a very reluctant Caro off with him.

Now that she found herself relatively private with the duke, Julia could not think of a thing to say that sounded the least bit beguiling.

"You are certainly an interesting young lady, Miss Allard."

"Oh? How so, Your Grace?" She looked up at him with a twinkle in her eye, relieved that he started the conversation.

"I would have wagered a good sum of money that, before this evening, you did not hold me in high regard," he said in a languid tone.

"And now you think I do not?" she teased, watching his left eyebrow lift at her words.

"I confess that you leave me curious. But if you have forgiven me for . . . er . . . our encounter in London last year, then I own I'd be excessively pleased."

Feeling as if she might choke on the words, Julia

made a great effort to smile up at him. "Of course I have, Your Grace. Did you not make the prettiest speech when you apologized to me? I understand completely that it was just a high-spirited lark. Please, do not give it another thought."

At the hint of a frown between his brows and the assessing light that entered his eyes, Julia wondered if she had done the thing too brown. Her heart skipped at the thought of giving herself away this early in the game.

"You are exceedingly generous. I wonder if I would be were I in your shoes."

"I'm sure you would be, but that's behind us now. Tell me, Your Grace, are you intending to stay in Bath for the Season?" She opened her fan and waved it in a languid manner, doing her best to gaze at him with avid interest.

He continued to look at her with a contemplative expression before answering.

"I believe I shall. Bath is quite restful compared to the feverish pace of London."

Shrugging lightly, she continued to wave her fan and attempted to keep her tone of voice airy. "I would not know." *Watch yourself, my girl, his left brow went up again.* She smiled at him to dispel any hint of coldness in her response.

"You do not like London?"

"I was only there a short while. But I very much like Bath, and have been having a delightful visit with my cousin and her husband."

"Lord and Lady Farren are indeed delightful; I am pleased to make their acquaintance. May I ask where you call home, Miss Allard?"

"I live on the outskirts of Chippenham, with my aunt and uncle. My uncle is not fond of being away from home, so I have come to visit Lord and Lady Farren without them."

"They must miss you."

"I hope so. But it is nice to be away. I shall have much to share when I return home."

"And what sorts of amusements have you discovered in Bath?"

"Any number of delightful entertainments. We ride, walk, visit, and shop. We go to parties and the assemblies at the Upper Rooms and to the Gardens when they have concerts." She finished, prodigiously pleased that he had not yet left her side.

"I believe there is going to be a special gala night at Sydney Gardens in honor of Princess Charlotte's wedding," the duke put in, smiling down at her.

"Yes, it promises to be memorable—they are planning a grand display of fireworks."

"Then hopefully we shall see each other there. But before then, would you care to join me in a carriage ride? We could go to one of the parks and indulge your love of walking."

"That would be delightful, Your Grace, thank you," she said, looking into his eyes, wondering at the hint of amusement lingering there.

"Would Thursday suit?"

"Perfectly."

"Until then," he said before bowing and leaving her side.

Watching his tall, broad-shouldered frame weave through the crowd, Julia's heart raced with exhilaration and fear.

Chapter Eleven

*G*aining the privacy of her bedchamber, Julia shut the door and leaned against it. With her eyes tightly closed, she relived those few moments of dancing with the duke and marveled. Could she truly have flirted with that dastard?

Pushing away from the door, she walked to the middle of the room and pressed her fingers to her hot cheeks. Catching sight of her reflection in the small looking glass on her dressing table, she was almost startled to see that her eyes were glowing with an unfamiliar intensity.

Hearing a knock, she whirled around to see Caro enter. Julia knew Caro would not be able to wait until morning to discuss the evening's events. On the way home, Caro had stared at her in concerned confusion while Clive chattered about how honored his mother was to have the duke and Lady Fallbrook grace her ball. Not wanting to say anything in front of Clive, Julia had remained silent during the drive home.

Now her eyes met her cousin's troubled gaze. Caro approached, her hands spread wide in supplication. "I thought my eyes were deceiving me when I saw the duke leading you to the floor. What in the world has caused you to change your opinion of him?"

A blush rose to Julia's cheeks. "Nothing."

"Nothing? Then why did you dance with him? Why were you behaving as if you welcomed his attention?" Caro's tone conveyed how baffled she felt at her cousin's inexplicable behavior.

Julia could not answer. For several moments the only sound in the room was the muted rustling of her gown as she paced the floor. Julia struggled for the words to explain her incongruent behavior.

Here, in the familiar coziness of her bedroom, her earlier behavior seemed unexplainable, her reasons unsupportable. Now she could scarce believe what she was contemplating.

Reaching the end of the room, she turned back and saw the concern plainly evident on her cousin's delicate features.

"Oh, Caro, I just could not stand it another moment."

"Stand what?"

"The Duke of Kelbourne! The way he is so insufferably sure of himself. I have tried to rise above my anger and forget. I might even have been able to if I had not met him again. But it is different now."

"But, Julia, he apologized to you, does that not count for something? Besides, what does this have to do with your surprising change of attitude this evening?"

"I do not know how to describe what happened. I saw him standing there, the lord of all he surveys, everyone practically bowing and scraping." Julia's tone took on a scathing edge. "All I could think of was how he had smiled when he apologized so flippantly to me. As I watched him tonight, I felt an overwhelming feeling of anger. I wanted more than anything to give him a taste of the damage he caused—to make him pay for his thoughtless arrogance. I kept thinking how I could have been ruined by his so-called lark. Because of his selfish actions, I have been gossiped about, and my aunt and uncle have been forced to prevaricate about my sudden return from London. My anger just kept growing. Of a sudden, inspiration struck and I realized I might be able to teach him a lesson after all."

"How?" Caro's tone was hushed with rapt attention, completely absorbed by the intensity of her cousin's emotions.

"He thought me pretty enough to use me to fulfill his bet—if I could capture his interest . . ."

"And make him fall in love with you and then break his heart!" Caro interjected sharply.

The look of shock on her cousin's face caused Julia an instant of shame.

She plowed ahead with a shake of her head. "The high-and-mighty Duke of Kelbourne would never allow himself to be so human as to fall in love. But I believe I can make him desire me."

"Desire!" Stunned, Caro slowly lowered herself on the dressing-table chair. "Julia, I have never heard you speak like this. You must stop this at once," she said, her voice rising in alarm.

"I know you are right, but I cannot. I feel I must see it through."

"But it is so reckless—so unlike you. What of your reputation? If you flirt too openly with the duke, you will be called fast."

"I do not care," Julia said, her jaw set with uncharacteristic defiance, and resumed her pacing. "My reputation is already in question because of him. Believe me, I do not take what I have started this evening lightly. I have never done anything so daring in my life. But as much as I shock myself, I must admit that I have no desire to stop."

"You astonish me! I hardly know you."

Julia turned earnest eyes to her troubled cousin. "Truly, Caro? Cannot you understand how I feel, at least a little bit?"

Biting her lip, Caro looked into her cousin's eyes. Julia held her breath in the tense silence. Caro's inner struggle was evidenced by her conflicted expression.

"You will not do anything truly foolish, will you?" Caro implored.

Suddenly very tired, Julia offered a wan smile. "In truth, I am not planning to do anything. He will likely go on to another lark, and this will all come to naught."

"I confess I hope that's true. But I must admit that I can understand how you feel—I am just worried that you will be hurt."

Moving to her cousin, Julia embraced her and gave a little laugh. "That man has hurt me once, I shall not let him do so again. Do not worry, I have no intention of doing anything too foolish. I am sure the best I can hope to do is prick his pride."

"Somehow, I think you are underestimating the risk you are taking. But we shall not speak of this anymore tonight." Caro kissed Julia's cheek and gave her one last concerned look before bidding good night.

After the door closed behind her cousin, Julia stood in the middle of her room for several moments, a frown between her brows as she contemplated what she had begun.

Lingering over a late breakfast the next morning, Julia was relieved to be alone with her thoughts. Earlier, Caro and Clive had invited her on an outing, but Julia had declined, preferring to spend the day quietly.

When she had almost completed her breakfast, the

butler brought in a letter and placed it next to her plate. Curiously, she opened the missive and read it with dawning pleasure.

At last, she whispered to herself, setting aside her napkin. Suddenly, the urge to see her friend propelled her out of the chair and back up the stairs. Sweeping into her room, she found her maid tidying things up.

"Harper, I shall need my blue gown, the new one with the fawn-colored pelisse. We are going to . . ."—she glanced down at the letter still in her hand—"York House. Mrs. Thorncroft and her daughter have taken rooms there, and I wish to visit them this morning."

"Very good, miss." Harper abandoned straightening the bedclothes and went to the wardrobe.

A short while later, with her maid in tow, Julia headed out the front door into the bright spring sun. In her great desire to see her friend, she did not bother to wait for the butler to call a carriage for her. Long strides took her up the cobbled street, and she took note that the sky was painted with a multitude of feathery white clouds. At least the day did not seem to be threatening rain.

Upon entering the elegant little inn, a man she assumed was the proprietor approached, bowed, and bid her good afternoon.

After acknowledging his greeting with an inclination of her head, Julia asked that Miss Thorncroft be informed of her arrival. "I am Miss Allard."

"Ah, Miss Allard," said the plump, well-dressed man. "Miss Thorncroft is expecting you. If you will come this way, I shall show you to the private sitting room, where Miss Thorncroft awaits you."

Following him down a short hallway, Julia thought it was just like her friend to instinctively know that Julia would come to her straightaway.

The man opened the door and announced Julia. Looking past him, Julia was relieved to see that Mariah was alone.

The man stood back, and Julia walked past him into the room with Harper close behind. After the man bowed himself out, Harper went to a chair in the far corner and took out her sewing bag. Julia rushed to where Mariah stood in front of the bow window, looking exquisite in a cream and lace gown, and embraced her old friend.

"Mariah, you have no notion of how glad I am that you are here! You must forgive me if I forgo the niceties and instantly tell you my news."

Pulling back, Mariah's eyes were alight with pleasure mingled with curiosity. "Yes, yes, sit next to me and tell me everything. I have been feeling very curious since your last letter, when you wrote that you had much to tell me that you did not want to put on paper."

They sat together on the settee, and Julia launched into her story, starting with the unexpected encounter with the duke at Sydney Gardens and ending with the ball at Lady Farren's last night. As she spoke, Julia watched the surprise and concern cross her friend's features.

"Good heavens! I am agog and scarce know what to say! Are you truly going to continue with your plan when you meet him the day after tomorrow?"

"Yes! As bad as it makes me seem, I want to teach him a lesson, if I can. Do you think I am awful?"

"Oh, my dear, do not be a goose! All these years we have known one another, you have been the truly good one. How many times have you discouraged me from some madcap scheme or another? You have always been everything prudent and wise. But this business with the insufferable duke is enough to try the fortitude of a saint. Besides, he deserves to be taught a lesson after what he did to you."

Relieved that she had the full support of her friend, Julia smiled to herself, marveling at the difference in Mariah's reaction compared to Caro's. Julia knew she should not have been surprised, for Mariah had always been up to every rig and row.

"Mariah, you must help me decide what to do next—I haven't the faintest notion of how to go on."

"Well, I don't have much of an idea either. I think you have done very well on your own."

"Yes, but I want to go about this the right way. I want him on his knees before me, so that I can turn my nose up and say, 'Oh, my dear duke, it was just a *lark*!' "

Mariah clapped her hands at this cunning plan and laughed at the haughty look Julia affected so well. "I know it's appalling to admit, but this is all so deliciously exciting. I cannot wait to see the look on the duke's face. This is a much more fitting revenge than boiling him in oil."

With a sigh, Julia relaxed against the settee cushions. "Only if it works. I admit he is paying attention, but that's a far cry from forming a *tendre* for me."

"I agree. Now, let us see . . ." Mariah tapped her chin in concentration. "My brothers become crazed if the ladies they are pursuing go for drives with other men, or waltz with someone else."

Julia contemplated Mariah's words. "Hmm, there are not very many eligible candidates to make him jealous. There is Mr. Dillingham, but as attractive as he is, he certainly is in no way a threat to someone like the duke."

"Well, I do not think it signifies that this Mr. Dillingham, or any other man for that matter, does not compare to the duke. The duke is so puffed up by his own consequence that he shall be driven to distraction by jealousy if, after showing a partiality to him, you suddenly behave as if you prefer someone else. But your plan will fizzle like damp fireworks if the duke is too sure of you—or if he gets the slightest hint of what you are about."

Julia looked at her friend with a hint of awe. "You are very good at this, Mariah. I do not know what I would do without you. What if, after our drive on Thursday, I am suddenly not at home to the illustrious Duke of Kelbourne?"

"Very good!" Mariah nodded her approval. "He shall wonder why you are not available to his delightful personage, and his conceit will drive him to pursue you more earnestly."

"Brilliant! I feel ever so much better now that you are here helping with my plan. I shall not think any further than Thursday, or I might lose my nerve."

"I think that is best. After your ride with the duke, we shall put our heads together again and decide what to do next."

Smiling, Julia sighed with relief. "Now, enough about my little drama. You must tell me how you managed to convince your mama to come here instead of going to London."

"It was not difficult at all. Since we really do not know anyone of any importance in London, once we received the invitation from Lady Farren, Mama was quite pleased to come to Bath."

"Good, then she will not be in any hurry to leave."

"Not at all. Please say you will stay for luncheon." Mariah's tone made it clear that she would not take no for an answer.

"I would be delighted. Will your mama be joining us?"

"Alas not, she is fatigued today and will probably not appear until dinner. Just as well, I think we should discuss how you are going to behave with the duke on Thursday."

"An excellent idea. I thought I might practice some of the flirtatious things I have thought of to say to the duke. I very much wish to be prepared."

"You are wise. That way they will sound more natural." Mariah smiled and added, "I have missed you. I do not care what the fashionable world says; Bath is wonderful and I know we shall have a merry time."

"Indeed," Julia said as a voice deep in the recesses of her heart whispered words of warning.

Chapter Twelve

"Please hurry, Harper, I wish to be in the salon when His Grace arrives."

"I am on the last button, miss," the maid said, her nimble fingers working quickly. "There!"

With a nod of thanks, Julia picked up her reticule and moved to the dressing table, making one last check of her appearance in the mirror.

She was pleased that she had taken Mariah's advice and worn the new mulberry-colored sarsenet walking dress and dove gray spencer. Several months ago, when Julia had the ensemble made, the dressmaker had stated that the treble quilling of satin ribbon at the cuffed sleeves was the height of fashion. Julia hoped so, for she felt it was imperative that she look smart.

After a final adjustment to her small-brimmed bonnet, she took a deep breath and left the room.

As she made her way downstairs toward the main salon, Julia decided that it was for the best that Clive had taken Caro off to make calls and visit his mother. If Caro had stayed, Julia feared that she might say something indiscreet in front of the duke.

As a child, Caro had always been cautious and,

because of her mother's tutelage, had a keen regard for the dictates of Society and was excessively attentive to all the proprieties.

Even this morning Caro had not been shy about cautioning Julia to behave prudently. Realizing that Caro was truly anxious about the duke, Julia had done her best to assure her cousin that her behavior would be all that was correct. Caro's expression showed her skepticism, but she had said nothing further on the matter.

For his part, Clive was no end pleased that the Duke of Kelbourne was calling on his guest. "Ho, ho, Cousin Julia, it is certainly a feather in your cap to have the duke pay you such marked attention."

Julia had affixed a smile to her lips. *Oh, yes, I'm so flattered that a proclaimed rakehell has shown me such condescension.* "I shall see you both at dinner," she had called to them as they left.

Upon entering the salon, she swiftly took in the room. *Would it be better to stand in front of the window or be seated on the settee next to the vase of irises?* The window, she decided, hurrying across the room, fearing the duke would be announced before she could position herself to the best advantage.

With her back to the door, she twisted this way and that until she felt satisfied that she was in the proper pose. She wanted the duke, upon entering, to see her gazing out the window, which overlooked the back garden, in an artless manner. This way, he would be met by the left side of her profile. When they had conspired together on Tuesday, Mariah assured her that her left side was her most attractive.

Despite the intense pounding of her heart, Julia felt a welcome sense of confidence. Her time with Mariah had put her at ease, and with her friend's support, Julia knew without shame that she would relish the revenge she now believed she was capable of exacting from the insufferable duke. It was, she reminded herself, only what he deserved.

The door opened, followed by the butler's sonorous announcement. "His Grace, the Duke of Kelbourne."

Instantly forgetting to take her time, she turned her head to see the duke filling the doorway. His disturbingly perceptive eyes instantly locked on hers.

For all her careful planning, she was not prepared for the unabashed air of masculinity that suddenly filled the room.

Lud, but he was attractive, she thought, so distracted that she forgot to present her profile.

Crossing the room, he doffed his hat before taking her hand in a brief salute. "Miss Allard, I thought the day was bright, but your beauty outshines the sun. And punctual as well? What other unexpected delights shall I discover as I come to know you?"

This was it, she thought, giving him her best smile. Just what she hoped for, a perfect opening to try one of the mildly provocative double entendres she had practiced on Mariah. His tone was so smooth, so laced with languid amusement that she fairly itched with the desire to take that overly confident expression off his face.

"Ah . . . thank you, Your Grace. May I offer you a refreshment, or would you rather not keep your horses standing?" She froze at hearing her own words. *Horses? Am I actually speaking of horses?*

"Thank you but no, Miss Allard. If you would not mind departing now, my cattle have been restless this afternoon."

"Of course, Your Grace." *Of course?* She almost rolled her eyes at her missish behavior as she moved past him to the door. To her complete dismay, all the witty comments she had practiced seemed to have vanished from her brain.

Once outside, she saw a pair of chestnut Thoroughbreds prancing impatiently, the boy at their heads seemed to be having a difficult time controlling the magnificent animals. To her surprise, they where hitched to a phaeton with bright red wheel spokes. She had not seen such an elegant vehicle since her brief stay in London—and never one with red spokes.

Julia halted next to the vehicle. She had never had the occasion to ride in a high-perch phaeton, and wondered how one climbed up with any poise.

Smoothly, the duke stepped next to her and, with a firm hand on her elbow, helped her up onto the conveyance. Walking around to the other side, he stepped up with ease.

Settling next to Julia, he picked up the ribbons before tossing a coin to the delighted boy.

With a quick flick of the reins, they shot forward. Smiling, Julia put a hand up to steady her bonnet. It was a novelty to be so high above the road.

Despite the dismal failure of her initial attempt at beguilement, she decided to give it another try. "What a wonderful conveyance this is, Your Grace. I feel as if we are flying. Is it terribly difficult to handle?" She batted her eyelashes at him, careful to heed Mariah's warning not to overdo it lest she appear as if she had a speck in her eye.

He shot her a grin. "Not to worry, I have not tipped it over yet."

Unable to hold his gaze, she made a show of looking at the passing scenery. It was a glorious day, with strips of vivid blue sky between the rows of townhouses as the duke expertly tooled the phaeton through the narrow, cobblestone streets.

"My, you certainly handle the ribbons well." If

outright flirting seemed beyond her ken, then mayhap fawning interest would suffice.

For her efforts, he tossed her a look that was rife with amusement. "Thank you. I thought it would be pleasant to drive to the Orange Grove."

"Oh, how lovely." *Zounds, I sound like the veriest loon.*

Desperation grew as she fruitlessly tried to think of something else to say that would further her cause. *How did one go about being fascinating and alluring?* she pondered, biting her lip.

When she and Mariah had discussed how Julia would behave with the duke, it had seemed so simple. Somehow, they had gotten it wrong. This was certainly going to be more difficult than Julia had imagined. Everything she said made her feel like a vapid ninny.

They turned onto a wider lane, and she realized that what she had not anticipated was the effect his presence seemed to have on her senses. Something about the knowing, slightly amused gleam in his eyes almost choked the practiced words of flirtation in her throat.

But she was not ready to give up just yet. She was not going to throw away this unexpected chance to make him pay for that kiss.

For the moment, she would refrain from saying anything else that sounded silly. Being the niece of a soldier had taught her something about strategy. When she met Mariah for tea later, they would have to reassess her methods.

"What sorts of things do you enjoy doing in Chippenham?"

She paused, using the fact that he was making another turn to consider her reply. It certainly would not help her appear fascinating or alluring to tell him of the pleasure she took in teaching children to read and write, or how she helped in the planning of the annual church bazaar.

"Oh, we have a merry time of it at home. Parties and picnics and amusements of all sorts. May I ask where you reside, Your Grace?" This was not the most creative thing to say, but she comforted herself with the knowledge that she was very new to this flirting business.

"My family home is in Kent."

"I have not had the pleasure of visiting that part of the country, though I understand it is beautiful."

"It may be said that I am partial, but I think the Vale of Kelbourne is the most beautiful place in all of England."

The note of sincerity in his deep voice was unmistakable, and caused Julia to glance at him in surprise. His open emotion regarding his home did not mesh with her conviction that he was a shallow libertine.

She could think of nothing to say in reply. For all her careful practicing with Mariah and her determination to win the duke's affection by whatever means she had at her disposal, Julia found herself frustratingly mute as she sat next to the duke.

Settling back against the butter-soft leather squabs, she berated herself for her sudden loss of confidence.

For his part, the duke seemed to find nothing amiss in her behavior, and he continued to make polite conversation.

After he steered the phaeton around a Bath chair, they entered the picturesque Pulteney Bridge.

A veil of unreality settled over Julia. For a full year her anger and resentment of this arrogant man had colored her life—to the point that he had no longer seemed real. But here he was, flesh and blood and effortlessly charming.

In the cool light of day, and without Mariah to join in her fantasy of revenge, Julia began to feel her plan of affixing the duke's regard was ill planned at best. Not that she intended to give up—it was inconceivable to set aside a year's worth of anger just because she was suddenly unsure how to go on.

Besides, there was something so assessing, so aware in the warm chestnut gaze he directed at her, she now was sure that he would instantly see through her efforts if she did not have a care.

Glancing again to the duke, she noticed for the first time something unyielding and implacable in the strength of his features. There was a stubbornness to his square chin and a sharp intelligence in his gaze that she had not previously taken into account.

Their brief encounter last year had given her the false impression that he was a dissipated libertine. Since she'd come to Bath, it was exceedingly clear that there was nothing dissipated about the Duke of Kelbourne. He was vital, handsome, and completely at ease with himself.

Because of the information Caro had passed on about his mistress—the mistress who had named the ruby he had given her after him—Julia began to feel that her feeble attempts at capturing his attention were laughable in comparison. She should have considered the fact that he lived in a sophisticated world far removed from her own.

Until she came up with a better plan, she felt unaccountably relieved to cease this inane lash-batting and simpering.

"May I ask how you are enjoying your time in Bath, Your Grace?" Now that she had settled her mind, she suddenly found her tongue.

Before answering, he cast his whip with such precision that the tip barely flicked his cattle's haunches.

"It is a fine town with much to admire, and I own I am fascinated by the excavation of the ancient Roman artifacts."

Smiling to herself at this diplomatic statement, Julia was struck by what he had left unsaid.

"But what of amusements and culture? Surely Bath pales against the bright allure of London?" The culture of gaming, she thought cynically.

"It is certainly not as lively as London, and a decent card game is scarce, but for all that, I'm finding my stay in Bath diverting."

At his mention of gambling her brow arched up. She could not let this comment pass. "Being well aware of your fondness for wagering, I am astonished that you would not find the poor gaming here reason enough to seek more exciting pastures."

Apparently, her blatant reference to his reason for kissing her last year startled the duke considerably; his horses actually lost their rhythm for a few strides. He cocked a brow in her direction and did not hide his surprised amusement. "My dear Miss Allard, you are a deep one. Here I thought, by unspoken agreement, those few moments on Bolton Street would not be brought up between us."

"You mistake me, sir. I was only referring to your love of gaming."

"And the only reason you have any knowledge of my so-called love of gaming is because I told you the ridiculous reason I stopped you that day."

She gave him a breezy nod. "Yes, that is true. And I am glad that you did. I was much relieved to know that you were fulfilling the terms of a wager. You see, for a year I assumed that you must have escaped your keeper."

The duke's deep laugh set the gooseflesh rising on her skin. "So, you prefer that the man who accosted you be a profligate gamester instead of just harebrained?"

"Would not you?" She found herself smiling back at him. At least he had the grace to call himself a profligate gamester.

They reached the Orange Grove, and as they pulled to a stop, Julia noticed a number of fashionably dressed people strolling among the perfectly aligned rows of trees.

A boy darted forward, kicking up gravel, asking the *"gov'ner"* if he wanted his horses held.

"Aye, lad, they should be spent enough for you to handle." The duke tossed the boy the ribbons and leapt agilely from the conveyance and then came around to assist Julia.

As she stood, she caught sight of the beautiful view of the ancient edifice of Bath Abbey, its majestic gothic spires rising high above the town.

Suddenly, Julia was pleased to be out-of-doors, even if it was in the company of the duke. Oddly, he did not seem so much like an enemy today as he solicitously helped her from the phaeton.

Once she reached the ground, he did not let go of her hand. Instead, he pulled it through the crook of his elbow as he led her to the walking path.

"Well, Miss Allard, now that you are assured I am not a half-wit, I propose that we walk in the sunshine and continue to get to know one another."

Something in the lazy confidence of his manner set her back up. "For people who shall be acquainted a short time, I am of the opinion that it is much better—and more interesting—to remain a mystery to each other."

His left brow arched. "Indeed? How singular. Why?"

"I have found that the occasional dance or walk in a park is quite enough between mere acquaintances. Often, any more than that causes the parties involved to grow bored with the inadequate glimpses of character that are revealed in so short a time together."

They walked a number of yards before he replied. "This opinion intrigues me. You do not believe that it is possible for some people to gain a true knowledge of each other in a short span of time?"

"Not for a deep or lasting friendship, Your Grace."

"Hmmm. So, you propose that we stroll along and discuss the weather?"

"That sounds perfectly agreeable." To her surprise, she quite enjoyed teasing him in this dry manner.

"Sounds deadly dull if you ask me."

"Compared to high-stakes gaming, I am sure it does. But some of us may have had enough excitement, and a quiet walk may be an adequate form of entertainment."

Slowing his gait, he looked down at her, a speculative light entering his eyes. "Ah, I have the measure of you now. Making veiled references to having too much excitement maintains the air of mystery you just alluded to. Well done, Miss Allard."

"How vexing of you to read something into my words I did not intend." She smiled softly to soften the rebuke.

"I beg forgiveness. I believe I have been vexing enough to you." He grinned and gave her a slight bow. "So, has not the weather been uncommon kind to us of late?"

Glancing up at the tease in his voice, she met the warm humor in his brown gaze. *Drat the man, what did he truly know of how he vexed her?*

"Yoo-hoo! Kel dear, over here!"

The duke stopped at hearing his name, and Julia turned to see two women and a young man approaching. The older woman waved a parasol; the younger lady was very pretty, with light brown hair, dark blue eyes, and a slim elegant carriage. Julia had to stop herself from staring at the gentleman, for she had never seen such a vibrant fop. His lime, yellow, and red-striped waistcoat was the most vivid thing she had witnessed since coming to Bath.

Turning to the gentleman, Julia was a little startled

to note that he was staring directly at her with the oddest expression. An inexplicable feeling of dread spread over her in a barely concealed shiver.

The three were upon the duke and Julia in an instant. The older woman spoke first. "Kel, why did you not tell me you would be here? Oh, it matters not. You will never guess whom I have found. Of course you can guess, silly me, for they are right in front of you. Look! Lady Davinia and Lord Mattonly have come to Bath! Is it not delightful?" On this breathless note, the lady gestured to the younger people next to her before turning curious eyes to Julia. "Kel, you may present this young lady."

Julia did not know what to make of this vivacious, attractive little woman, who reminded her of Mariah's frisky little terrier.

"Maman, I would like to present Miss Allard." The duke turned to Julia. "This is my mother, the Duchess of Kelbourne, and our very good friends, Lady Davinia Harwich and Lord Mattonly."

Julia curtsied, but before she could voice a greeting, the duchess was off again. "Miss Allard? I do not believe we have met. Tell me, how do you know my son?"

"We were introduced by mutual friends, Maman." The duke put in smoothly before Julia could respond.

Lord Mattonly frowned at this statement, his eyes still on Julia. "What? Here in Bath? I say, Miss Allard, did we not meet in London last year? 'Pon my word, you do look familiar to me."

Julia opened her mouth to disagree, when a sudden memory of four men following the duke across Bolton Street, before he kissed her last year, flashed into mind. She felt her cheeks growing hot as her mind grasped the fact that Lord Mattonly had been one of those men.

Chapter Thirteen

*J*ulia's arrested expression and flushed cheeks caught the duke's attention. Frowning, he shifted his gaze back to Mattonly.

He realized it would not take long for Matt to recognize Julia as the young woman Kel had kissed in London. It would not do to have his wagered kiss brought up at this wholly inappropriate time. For now, until he could gain a moment of privacy with Matt to tell him to put a stopper in it, he would have to take the situation in hand.

Stepping smoothly into the breach of silence, he sent Julia what he hoped was a reassuring smile and said, "Yes, I believe you were in London last Season, were you not, Miss Allard? Quite possible you and old Matt met at some crush or other."

"Yes, I was in London for a short time last year." Shaken that the duke's friend could so easily expose her in front of the duchess and Lady Davinia, her resentment flared anew at the injustice of it all. For even though she was a complete innocent in the matter, she would be the only one to pay for the duke's lark.

"That explains it," he said, then turned back to his friend. "I am surprised to find you here, Matt." The duke's delusory tone did not convey pleasure in his old friend's company.

"If Muhammad won't come to the mountain . . . Besides, Town is dashed dull right now. All anyone can speak of is the upcoming royal wedding. Since you suddenly find Bath all the crack, I thought I would toddle over and see what you are about. Maybe we can bring Bath back into fashion, eh, Kel?" Lord Mattonly's eyes shifted to Julia again. " 'Tis frustrating not to be able to place you, Miss Allard, for your face is extremely familiar to me—oh, well, no doubt it shall come to me."

The duke turned to the other young lady with the intent of changing the subject. "Lady Davinia, how are your parents? Are they in Bath as well?"

"No, Your Grace, I am visiting my Aunt Harwich and am finding this quaint town a delight. And my parents are quite well, thank you."

The duchess stepped forward then, waving her hands in a gesture that encompassed them all. "Well, are we not a merry party? But I must say, I am disappointed that there are no orange trees here. Why in the world call this place the Orange Grove? Silliest thing I have ever encountered."

At this, Julia's gaze inadvertently met Lady Davinia's, and the look they exchanged conveyed to Julia that she was not the only one trying to stifle a giggle.

"This place is named after William of Orange, Maman. There is a plaque on that obelisk over there indicating so." With great patience, he gestured to the circular garden in the center of the grove.

"Oh, well, that explains it. Still rather confusing. Now, what shall we all do?" Her smile took in the whole group.

"Actually, Miss Allard and I . . ." the duke began.

"We shall all promenade with the other Fashionables while I wrack my brainbox trying to recall where Miss Allard and I have met," Lord Mattonly interrupted with an engaging grin to Julia.

Setting his jaw with frustration, Kel shot Julian an apologetic look.

"Lovely." Lady Davinia's smile showed her pleasure at this plan as she gazed up at the duke. "We have not seen each other since New Year's. We must catch up on all the friends we have in common."

Lord Mattonly vigorously nodded his agreement to this suggestion. "Fine! While you old friends catch up on gossip, Her Grace and I shall quiz Miss Allard. I never forget a Beauty, and this is vexing me no end that I cannot place her."

In spite of the razor-sharp look Kel sent his friend, Mattonly adroitly insinuated himself between Julia and the duke.

The duchess and Lady Davinia moved forward, but stopped quickly and looked back in surprise when they realized the duke and Miss Allard were still behind.

"Come along, now that we have found each other we must all walk together. I do so love to have young folks around me," the duchess pressed.

In the face of the duchess's urging, Julia knew there was nothing else for it but to go along, anything else would be rude. With an inward sigh of resignation, Julia continued next to the duke as his mother moved to his other side. Lady Davinia took her place next to the duchess. Lord Mattonly stayed near Julia.

In silent accord, the five of them began to stroll along the gravel pathway between the precisely spaced trees.

Breathing deeply, Julia tried to stem the flow of her rising panic. Oh, why had she been so foolish as to go out with the duke, she chided herself.

"Perhaps I am acquainted with your family?" Lord Mattonly asked after a moment.

"I have lived near Chippenham all my life, sir."

"Hmmm, have only had the pleasure of passing through that village. And I own I am not acquainted with anyone by the name of Allard. Perhaps there is another connection?"

"I am visiting my cousins, Lord and Lady Farren. Perhaps you know them?"

Pulling a gold quizzing glass from his vibrantly striped waistcoat, he began to tap it absentmindedly against his palm. "Farren? I believe my mama is acquainted with Lady Farren. Does not Lady Farren wear very interesting bonnets?"

"I am sure you must be referring to the dowager Lady Farren. I am related to her daughter-in-law."

"Then that must somehow be the connection! Still, it has not come to me in full. But I shall not give up," he said with a grin as they all strolled beneath the trees.

Tilting her head up, Julia looked at the handsome lord. With his twinkling pale blue eyes and sandy hair, he presented an engaging figure. Nevertheless, she had no desire to be quizzed about where they had met. What she really wanted to do was go home—she had not bargained for this uncomfortable encounter with the duke's mother and his friends.

As they continued to walk, the duchess and Lady Davinia monopolized most of the conversation, to Julia's great relief. At least the friendly chatter prevented Lord Mattonly from asking any more questions.

Leaning forward, the duchess looked past her son and smiled at Julia. "Miss Allard, I have just realized that my mother-in-law is a great good friend of your cousin's mother-in-law. We have invited the Farrens to join us at Sydney Gardens Tuesday next. You must certainly honor us with your presence as well. The orchestra is very good, and if the weather stays fine, it promises to be a lovely evening."

"I thank you, Your Grace," Julia said with an inclination of her head, for she could think of no way to decline the kind invitation with any politeness.

"Very good!" Lord Mattonly exclaimed. "I must spend as much time as possible with Miss Allard, so that I may place our connection."

"Unfortunately, you will not be spending any more time with Miss Allard this afternoon. I promised to return her home shortly, in time for another engagement." The duke's tone conveyed that he would brook no argument.

Julia could not help but throw him a grateful glance at this almost intuitive understanding of her desire to leave.

"Never say so! I have not had the chance to talk with Miss Allard." Lady Davinia gave Julia a tentative smile, which Julia returned easily.

Despite the general protests at their departure, and promises to meet again, the duke lead her away after she offered a quick curtsy. Glancing back over her shoulder, she saw Lord Mattonly watching her with slightly narrowed eyes.

Once back in the phaeton, she was keenly aware of the same deflated feeling she experienced when she had been sent home from London. It was a feeling she did not like.

What a disaster the day had been. It started out with such promise and then fizzled to nothing. Again, her unvented resentment made her feel petulant. Even that caused her anger to simmer anew at the duke—this unpleasant emotion would not be plaguing her if not for him.

They traveled some distance in silence before the duke came to a decision. He thought it would be best to address the situation forthrightly and set her mind at ease.

At a turn in the road, he sent her a reassuring smile. "Miss Allard, I will explain to Lord Mattonly that he is not to refer to the incident on Bolton Street. I would be immensely distressed if you suffered any ill effects from that foolish lark." Smiling slightly, he took another moment to glance at her features.

The change in her expression took him aback. From beneath her bonnet, she was staring at him with such anger that her gray eyes flashed fire until he felt almost scorched.

"How magnanimous of you, Your Grace," was her cold response.

To the Duke of Kelbourne's surprise, Miss Allard said not a word, nor looked in his direction, the rest of the way home.

Chapter Fourteen

The next day, at an hour too early to be considered fashionable, Lord Mattonly called on his old friend at the Royal Crescent. Upon finding the duke alone in the salon, attending to a stack of correspondence, Mattonly brought up the subject that had been on his mind since yesterday.

"I say, Kel, Miss Allard is a deuced pretty gel. Leave it to you to find the only entrancing female in this damned dull place."

Pushing aside his quill and paper, Kel looked at his friend with an impassive expression, and leaned back in his chair.

"And good afternoon to you, Matt. How are you this fine day?"

Flopping onto a nearby chair, Mattonly snorted before responding.

"Cast your cold eye upon me all you like, you will not divert me from the subject of Miss Allard. I have the feeling you are being sly about her, but I shall winkle it out of you. I am determined to solve the mystery of Miss Allard's familiar countenance."

"There is no mystery where Miss Allard is concerned. She is familiar to you because she is the young lady I kissed on the street in London last year.

I would not like that ridiculous scene mentioned again; it would not do to have Miss Allard embarrassed. I have come to know that she and her family are fine people, and I would not like anything I have done to cause her pain."

Pushing himself forward, Mattonly stared, his mouth opening and closing before he collected himself enough to speak. "I am all astonishment, Kel! For weeks Rayburn, Hammond, and the rest of us scoured London for that girl. The sums wagered on finding her are a ransom! And there is no time limit on when the wager could be concluded. I am sure if I had not been foxed that day in London, I would have recognized her straight off yesterday. Are you now saying I am to pass on the winnings because some unexpected streak of scruples has gripped you? Too mean of you, old man."

"This is not another lark, Matt. I would prefer that the incident not be mentioned again."

Lord Mattonly could not mistake the serious edge in his old friend's voice.

"Of course, Kel, the matter is forgotten."

"Thank you."

Clearing his throat, Mattonly settled back in his chair. "So, how long do you plan on staying in Bath?"

Kel crossed his legs at the ankles and shrugged. "I have not decided. As long as I am amused, I shall linger. By the by, what has caused you to descend upon me?"

"You, of course," Mattonly said with a shrug. "It pains me to say so, but without you there to kick up my heels with, I find London dashed dull. Come, Kel, what say you? Let's quit this dreary hamlet and find something to stir up the blood."

Kel shifted again and appeared to think while Mattonly waited hopefully.

"I think not."

To this, Matt gave a disgusted snort. "The more important question is why you are here. The vision of you standing in line at the Pump Room with cits and dowagers does not sit well."

Kel gave a light shrug of amusement. "I'm indulging my sister's desire to have me here. Bath reminds Maman and Grandmère of their younger days, when Bath was all the crack. We have not spent much time together of late. Several weeks in their company is a pleasant enough way to spend the spring."

"I commend you on being such an attentive son and good brother," Mattonly said with a sly grin. "I shall keep myself here also. Though it ain't London, there may be some amusement to be had here after all. No matter what you say, I suspect the lovely Miss Allard may be one of your reasons for staying."

Kel gave a dismissive bark of laughter. "There may be a grain of truth in what you say. For all her beauty—and I admit she is exceedingly beautiful— Miss Allard is a peculiar minx. One moment batting her lashes and hanging on my every word, and the next looking as if she would take great delight in skewering me."

"You don't say."

"Indeed. I usually have little time for changeable misses, but I do find Miss Allard's fits and starts diverting for the moment—if only to see what she will do next. You are correct in saying Bath is not London, but it amuses."

At that moment, Julia was in the salon of her cousin's townhouse, conveying yesterday's events to Caro and Mariah Thorncroft, who sat in rapt attention, watching Julia pace back and forth.

"And then to cap it off, he says to me, 'I will tell Mattonly that he is not to mention the incident on Bolton

Street. I would be immensely distressed if you suffered any ill effects from that foolish lark.' " She deepened her voice to a gravely pitch, mimicking the duke.

Mariah snorted, and Caro bit her lip and said, "Oh my."

Julia continued to pace the room, throwing her hands up in disgust.

"Could anyone be more odious or insufferable? I am almost as angry with myself. Oh, Mariah, when I think of all the clever things you helped me think of—I could cry, for they all flew from my head. I must be the most inept flirt there ever was. But I am more determined than ever to get my revenge. I must regroup and determine where I went wrong."

"Do not you think it would be best to abandon this dangerous plan before it goes further?" Caro asked, a deep frown creasing her forehead.

"No," Julia stated flatly, continuing to pace.

Caro and Mariah exchanged glances.

"She has always been stubborn," Mariah said with a light shrug.

" 'Tis true," Caro sighed with a nod. "And because she came to my aunt and uncle rather late in their lives—in essence she is an only child—they rather spoiled her. So I daresay part of her vexation is because she has not gotten her way with the duke."

Mariah considered this statement while Julia glared fiercely at her cousin and continued to pace.

"I do not know if I agree with your assessment, Caro," Mariah said with a troubled frown. "I have always known her to be a most generous and thoughtful creature. I would say she is more willful than truly spoiled."

"Indeed, you may be correct," Caro conceded. "But I fear being stubborn and willful may get her into trouble in this matter."

"Would the two of you like me to leave the room

so you may continue to malign my character in private? I believe that is how it is usually done." Julia's tone oozed sarcasm.

"Do not bestir yourself, m'dear, we shall not let your presence stop us." Mariah gave her old friend a mischievous grin.

"Well, neither of you are any help. How am I to regain my footing where the duke is concerned?"

"I know you are used to being very popular in Chippenham, but His Grace is used to much more sophisticated ladies. If only you had developed a little more Town polish, you might not have been so easily thrown by a man of the duke's consequence," Caro offered.

Julia stopped her pacing to look askance at her cousin. "My dear Caro, are you off your head? If I do not have any Town polish, as you put it, you can put the blame for it at the duke's door."

"That is true," Mariah put in. "You cannot know what it was like for Julia this past year. There has been so much gossip about her in the village. She has had no real way of defending herself. If she assuaged the curiosity by telling everyone what happened, there would be those who would still twist it around to make it appear as if Julia goes around kissing men on the street. Besides, who would take Julia's side against a duke of the realm? No, I do not blame Julia for wanting to exact a bit of revenge."

"Thank you, Mariah, though I hardly feel any better."

"Well, I may not have said it very delicately, but you know what I mean."

"Did you say that Lady Davinia Harwich was part of the party yesterday?" Caro asked of Julia.

"Yes, she seemed a very amiable and pretty young lady," Julia responded as she finally lowered herself into a chair facing the two other ladies.

"Well, if you are determined to continue with this ill-conceived plan to capture the duke's regard, you may have a problem there," Caro said.

"How so?"

"It has been a common rumor for several years now, that once Kel is done sowing his oats, he will marry Lady Davinia. The families are well acquainted, and I believe part of the duke's estate marches with the Harwichs'."

Julia frowned at this information as she tried to recall how the duke and Lady Davinia behaved together.

"My impression of their relationship is that of childhood friends. I allow that would not preclude an understanding between them. Often in great families, alliances are created on less than such a connection. But as there is no engagement, I do not think I shall worry about it."

Caro shifted uncomfortably in her seat. "Let us call a turnip a turnip. What you are planning to do is tease the duke into desiring you and then laugh in his face. That is a very dangerous game, Julia."

"Yes, I know it is." Julia felt the blush rising to her cheeks at her cousin's bald assessment of her intentions.

"Although I am a year younger than you are, I am married and therefore have a superior understanding of how men and women behave together in private. I have learned that a woman, by using her powers of femininity, dare I say, powers of seduction, can cause a man to lose his head. I have found it to be a very heady feeling indeed."

Startled, Julia looked from Caro to a wide-eyed Mariah, then back to her cousin. "I have no intention of allowing the situation to get out of hand."

A mysterious smile came to Caro's lips. "I caution

you to have a care—while you are trying to make
the duke lose his head, you may well lose yours."

"I shall take great care." Julia's tone was very serious in response to Caro's unexpected disclosures.

"I know there has been talk about you, yet nothing
can be stated as fact. But Bath exists on gossip. You
may well lose the regard of some worthy gentleman
in the future if your unguarded behavior with the
duke becomes known."

"I do not care."

"But what of your future?"

Julia sighed. "Caro, I am four and twenty, not a
little girl pinning my hopes on the dream of a knight
arriving on my doorstep. I have a very happy and
useful life in Chippenham. If I never marry, so be it.
I shall continue with my aunt and uncle. I shall sew
clothes for the poor, sing in church, and continue to
teach some of the village children to read and write.
And when you have children, you may leave them
with me on occasion so that you and Clive may go
to Town and pretend you are newlyweds again. Rest
assured, I intend to be perfectly content with my
life."

"What of our aunt and uncle? You know they
would be appalled at your behavior."

"Yes, they would. It pains me, and do not think I
am proud of what I am doing. But Aunt Beryl and
Uncle John are not fully aware of how I feel, or what
it has been like in the village this past year. I have
not told them of some of the slights and insults I
have received, because I know it would just cause
them pain. Believe me, I am sensible of the risk I
am taking."

"Then there is nothing I can say to dissuade you
in this reckless plan?"

"I am afraid not, dear cousin."

"See, willful and stubborn," Caro sighed with a woeful shake of her head to Mariah, who nodded her agreement.

Julia looked from one to the other, her expression a mixture of indignation and affection. "Really! Have the two of you forgotten that I know you just as well as you know me? Caro, I seem to recall a fine vase being broken in your mother's boudoir a number of years ago, and you swearing me to secrecy as to how it came to be broken. And, Mariah, do you recall beseeching me to procure an ink pot for you so that you could play a rather cruel prank upon one of your brothers?"

Caro and Mariah exchanged surprised, yet amused, glances. "As you said, Mariah, our Julia is the most generous and thoughtful of creatures! Now, shall I ring for tea?"

Chapter Fifteen

By mid-afternoon on Tuesday, a dense, low cloud cover hung over the sloping hills of Bath. Caro, ever the optimist, looked out of the salon window and cheerfully pronounced that it would serve as a pleasing backdrop to the fireworks display planned for the evening's entertainment at Sydney Gardens.

Now, as her maid helped her put the finishing touches to her toilette, Julia fretted over how to behave with the duke.

For several days she had been feeling an inexorable escalation of tension building within her at the thought of seeing the duke again. As promised, the duke's mother had sent an invitation to join her party at Sydney Gardens. Julia had accepted promptly and, over tea, had urged Mariah to come also.

"I know it promises to be a dreadful crush, but you and your mama must come. If you arrange it artfully, it will appear as if you are just happening by. I shall be ever so pleased to see you and will make the introductions. The duchess, with her impeccable manners, shall invite you and your mama to join us."

Mariah had agreed to this plan instantly. "Even if it does not work out to your specifications, I should still like to attend the gala night. It sounds a lovely way to spend an evening."

"Good, it is settled, then. We shall see you there," Julia had said with satisfaction. But that was the last moment of satisfaction she had felt since.

Two days after the visit to the Orange Grove, Julia, Mariah, and Mrs. Thorncroft returned to the townhouse after an afternoon of shopping. Upon entering the foyer, the butler, Hill, informed her that the Duke of Kelbourne had called while she was out.

Julia had exchanged a startled glance with Mariah as Mrs. Thorncroft vigorously fanned herself with her handkerchief. "Bless me! Mariah dear, I think I need my hartshorn. To think a duke of the realm has called upon our dearest Julia! Mariah, you must endeavor to emulate Julia, for she is certainly doing something right!"

Recalling this now, Julia made a wry face at herself in the mirror. She certainly did not feel as if she was doing anything right. After their last encounter, it was obvious that flirting with the duke was much easier in theory than in actuality. Blast him, when he looked at her with that knowing, amused glint in his eyes, every clever thing she wanted to say shriveled up and blew away.

Frowning, she remembered the nasty things Mr. Fredericks had said to her, and the veiled innuendos Mrs. March had spread through the village. Again, her wounded pride gnawed at her.

Glancing at the clock on the mantel, Julia quickly completed her toilette. From her brief acquaintance with Clive, she knew he was a stickler for punctuality.

Gathering her large, deep green shawl and reticule, she checked her appearance one last time. Without vanity, she knew the deep violet blue of her gown did wonderful things for her pale complexion. She only hoped the duke would think so, too.

Moments later, as a smiling Clive handed her in the coach, Julia was glad of Caro's excited chatter, for it gave her a few moments to gather her composure. Heavens, she was nervous, she thought as the coach lurched to a start.

When they arrived at Sydney Gardens, Julia noticed the throngs of people—of every level of society—crowding around the entry.

"How shall we ever find the Kelbournes in this crush?" Caro looked crestfallen as her husband helped her from the carriage.

They need not have worried, for the moment they were all down from the coach, two footmen, dressed in burgundy and gray livery, approached and bowed in unison.

"His Grace, the Duke of Kelbourne, sends his felicitations. If you please, come this way," the older one said.

Julia exchanged a glance with Caro, and the look on her cousin's face showed how impressed she was with this attention.

"Very good," Clive said, offering Caro his right arm. Julia followed.

As the group made their way through the crowded garden, the tall footmen took care that the Farrens and Julia were close behind. As they walked up a meandering path, Julia looked ahead, through the trees and past the milling crowds, and saw an elegant stone pavilion. The sky was deep azure, and even though it would not be full dark for some time, she noticed the multitude of fairy lights that illuminated the paths, trees, and lush flower beds.

A vibration of excitement traveled through the very air, and Julia was aware of her own mounting

sense of excitement as they weaved their way
through the dense throngs of merrymakers. The
breadth of the footmen's shoulders and the consequence of their livery seemed to part the crowd
with ease.

They left the path and moved up to a flat area of
lawn near the pavilion, which afforded a sweeping
vista of the rest of the park and a clear view of the
orchestra below, several hundred yards away.

Although anyone was free to enjoy the garden for
the price of admittance, it was apparent to Julia that
the duke had claimed, in essence, this area for his
party. A large number of people mingled on the
grass, and footmen were setting up chairs and arranging cushions for the comfort of the guests. A
dozen or so blazing torches encircled the area, suc-
cessfully creating a certain illusion of privacy.

Gazing around with a smile, Julia saw the lights of
town beginning to twinkle in the distance as the fading
sun spread before her. The whole scene reminded her
of some romantic version of a medieval fair.

"My, the Kelbournes entertain in such state and
elegant opulence—I hardly know how to behave,"
Caro said, her tone filled with awe.

As the footmen led them within the circle of
torches, Julia's eyes instantly found the duke. With a
nervous gulp, she tried to slow her breathing. It was
not just his superior height and athletic build that
made him stand out. Her attention was caught by
something else altogether—the confidence and resolve displayed so plainly on his countenance.

Again, she was struck by how vital and handsome
he looked. His appearance was in complete contrast to
the ogre her imagination had created this past year.

He stood with his sister, Lady Fallbrook, and Lord
Mattonly. The duke's expression showed that he was

listening attentively, with no sign of condescension or impatience.

How amiable and easily charming he could be, she thought as she and the Farrens drew nearer—and how thoughtless and arrogant. The oddest touch of sadness mixed with her deep resentment of him.

More than anything, she wanted to cause him pain, to prick the mantle of pride and superiority he wore so well. She wanted to affect his life the way he had affected hers.

Of course, she knew powerful men like the duke could not be truly damaged. But even a fleabite could annoy, she thought, a half-smile rising to her lips at the thought. Satisfaction was what she was seeking; she could not seem to set aside her thoughts of revenge no matter how she rebuked herself.

Somehow, she knew she would have no peace until she hurt him. This unkind and unladylike thought caused her a stab of shame, but she resolutely pushed the unwanted emotion aside. She knew her own nature, and as long as she had the hope of capturing the duke's attention, she would keep trying—all so she could finally put to rest her desire for revenge.

The duke turned at that moment, and Julia experienced an unexpected thrill at the smile he sent her.

"Lord and Lady Farren. Miss Allard. We are pleased you could join us this evening. The weather has been kind to us, has it not?"

Julia sucked in her breath at the teasing, intimate smile he sent her. Obviously, his comment referred back to their previous conversation at the Orange Grove. She felt a little shock of surprise that he was not going to refer to her coldness toward him as he had driven her home.

"Yes, it is a lovely evening," she responded a little breathlessly.

His smile held hers for a moment before he turned to the others. "All of you are acquainted with my sister. But I do not believe Lord and Lady Farren have met Lord Mattonly."

As the duke performed the introductions in the light of the torches, she sighed at the ethereal beauty of the gloaming and admired the elegance of the other guests.

The sight of the duke's grandmother standing a little distance away with several ladies caught her attention. Studying the lady, Julia decided that the duke, in physical appearance, was more like his grandmother than his mother.

The duchess looked over at that moment and beckoned Julia with an imperious wave of her hand.

Eyebrows rising in surprise, Julia sketched a brief curtsy to the duke and the others before crossing the lawn to the duchess.

"Miss Julia Allard, how good of you to join us this evening. A few young faces are welcome."

Dipping into her best curtsy, Julia lowered her head. "Thank you, Your Grace."

"Let me make known to you my friends. Mrs. Sheldon, Mrs. Brent, and Miss Brent."

Julia curtsied to the three other ladies and wondered at the duchess paying her such marked attention. Mrs. Brent and Mrs. Sheldon looked to be the same age as the duchess. Miss Brent was an extremely thin, middle-aged woman who barely returned Julia's smile.

"Miss Allard is from Chippenham, I believe. She is an interesting creature, for I spent more than an hour in her company some days ago and she spoke nary a word about herself. Most singular compared to other young ladies of my acquaintance."

A footman approaching with a tray of wineglasses saved Julia from having to respond immediately to the duchess's startling comment.

Accepting a crystal goblet from the servant, Julia glanced at the duchess and was relieved, yet somewhat puzzled, by the glint of amusement dancing in the lady's hazel eyes.

"Do you find young ladies interesting as long as they say little, Your Grace?" Something in the mischievous gleam in the formidable lady's gaze convinced her that the duchess would not take offense at her pert reply.

The duchess gave a delighted laugh. "Saucy girl! But I confess you are correct. Most fashionable young women are tedious in the way they prattle on about themselves. I also find you unique in the fact that you seem to prefer the quiet charm of Bath to the excitement of London."

"But Bath is quite exciting of late, Your Grace," Mrs. Sheldon spoke up. "Now that your grandson indulges us with his presence, and some of his friends have come. Why, I believe Bath shall soon be just as fashionable as Brighton."

"Oh, tosh. My grandson can barely stay awake since he arrived in Bath. I am surprised he has not resorted to arranging a pugilist match in the Pump Room or setting the Upper Rooms on fire, just to relieve his boredom. Every morning, I confess myself astonished that he has not sneaked off to London in the middle of the night."

Julia hid her smile behind her glass while Mrs. Brent nodded her agreement. "Yes, having known your grandson for years, I am surprised he tolerates this quiet town. He's always been so full of high spirits; London seems the place for him."

The duchess snorted. "High spirits! How delicately put, Mrs. Brent. But you know as well as I that my grandson is a shocking rake."

At this, Julia almost choked on her wine. The duchess sent her a keen glance.

"Why do you look so astonished, Miss Allard? But I forget, you have spent little time in London. 'Tis no secret that my grandson leaps from one scrape to the next. Those dreadful gossip columns in Town are always full of his escapades."

"Indeed?" Julia replied quietly, at a loss as to how to respond to the duchess. She certainly could not tell the duchess how personally aware she was of the duke's "high spirits." At this thought, Julia stifled a laugh as she imagined what the lady's expression would be if she learned of what had happened on Bolton Street last year.

"Do not mistake me," the duchess said, wagging her finger. "My grandson is exceedingly attentive to all his duties. He has never failed his family, or the Crown. Indeed, my grandson's excellent management of his estates during the war was exemplary. But he inherited the title much too young, being only fourteen, and I think the burden wears on him at times. So I do not censure him for kicking up his heels a bit."

Julia took note of the deeply affectionate tone in the duchess's voice. But it was curious that the lady would be so open about such personal matters. Julia also found it curious the duchess would consider the mantle of nobility a burden to her grandson. Before this moment, Julia had only considered the privileges of a title, not the duties.

At that moment, the duke's mother approached. As she curtsied, Julia thought the lady seemed to glow like a jewel in her garnet-colored gown.

"Ah, Miss Allard, I am pleased to see that you have joined us on this fine eve. Has not my son arranged everything perfectly for our enjoyment? Mrs. Sheldon! Mrs. Brent! I did not see you, how do you do?"

As the duke's mother exchanged pleasantries with

the other ladies, Julia gazed around with interest. Possibly two dozen people mingled within the ring of torches, not including the servants. She observed the dowager Lady Farren sitting with Caro and Clive some little distance away. At least Caro appeared to be enjoying herself, Julia thought wryly. Indeed, on such a night, Julia doubted anyone could find fault— even with the dowager Lady Farren.

Her eyes continued to scan those assembled on the lawn until she came across the duke. He was obviously holding court, surrounded by a half a dozen people. Lady Davinia Harwich was included in their number, and by the laughing expression on her pretty features, she was evidently taking great delight in whatever the duke was saying.

Recalling what Caro had said about Lady Davinia, Julia wondered how much truth there was to the rumor that she would soon wed the duke. He certainly did not seem to be singling out the lady for any special attention.

Feeling a flutter in her chest, Julia kept her eyes on the duke for a moment. He would be busy mingling among the guests, so it might be difficult to attempt to say some of the alluring things she had practiced. Even so, she could not set aside her sense of breathless anticipation.

A movement from the other side of the duke caught her attention. Beyond the grassy area claimed by the duke for his guests, Julia saw Mariah and her mother hesitantly trying to gain her attention.

Smiling, she excused herself from the duke's mother and grandmother and moved across the lawn with a quick step.

"Mariah, Mrs. Thorncroft! How pleased I am to see you." She exchanged a warm glance with her childhood friend.

Mrs. Thorncroft took in the scene with wide eyes.

"Goodness! Oh my! Look at the gowns and jewels! You are certainly flying in high circles, Julia!"

Exchanging a quick glance with her friend, Julia saw that Mariah looked uncomfortable with the way her mother was gaping at the guests.

Glancing back, Julia caught Caro's eye and gave her a slight nod. A moment later Caro and Clive approached, with the dowager Lady Farren in tow.

"Mariah, Mrs. Thorncroft, how good to see you!" Caro smiled, and then made the introductions.

"How pleased we are to make your acquaintance, my lord, my lady," Mrs. Thornton gushed as she curtsied to Lord Farren and his mother. "Caroline, er, Lady Farren has always been very dear to us. We have watched with delight as she has grown into a very elegant and accomplished young lady. Over the years, my daughter and I always looked forward to the times when Caroline and her family would visit Chippenham."

"I am gratified that my daughter-in-law has such good friends," Clive's mother said in a neutral tone.

"And I am very glad to meet you both," Clive put in with a gracious smile. "My wife has told me of her pleasure in your company, Mrs. Thorncroft, Miss Thorncroft."

"You are very good, sir." Mrs. Thorncroft's face showed her gratification at this attention.

Julia could practically feel the palpable excitement throbbing from Mrs. Thorncroft. All of Chippenham knew that Mrs. Thorncroft was a desperate social climber, and Mariah often complained bitterly to Julia about how often her mother's desire to foist herself on the nobility often produced embarrassing results.

"Won't you introduce me to your friends, Miss Allard?" At the sound of the duke's deep voice, Julia gave a start.

Everyone looked at Julia expectantly. For a moment she was so taken aback by the duke's unexpected and disturbing presence, she could not speak.

"O-of course, Your Grace. This is Mrs. Thorncroft and Miss Thorncroft, my very good friends from Chippenham."

Mariah and her mother curtsied deeply as the duke gave a brief bow.

"I hope you will join us this evening. We shall have a perfect view of the fireworks from this spot."

Julia could not prevent a stunned glance to the duke. This invitation was most unexpected.

Mrs. Thorncroft gaped and stuttered, and Julia forced herself not to look at Mariah, for she knew they would both burst into laughter if she did.

"Thank you! We are most gratified by your invitation, Your Grace, are we not, Mariah?"

After a few more niceties, the duke excused himself to attend to some of the other guests. Julia's gaze met Mariah's in shared amusement at how Mrs. Thorncroft continued to flush and stutter.

Tonight must seem like a culmination of a long cherished dream for her dear friend's mother, Julia thought with gentle amusement. She watched the dowager Lady Farren lead the newcomers off to meet some of the other guests.

Julia deliberately hung back, for she desired a moment to think.

Moving to the edge of the grassy area, she had an unobstructed view of the orchestra. A moment passed before Julia heard the swelling of stringed and woodwind instruments.

For a little time, she stood there as the wave of musical notes enveloped her. As the melody began to fade, Julia saw from the corner of her eye the duke making his way toward her. Keeping her gaze fixed ahead, she felt the beat of her heart speed to a gallop.

"I trust you are enjoying yourself, Miss Allard?"

"Very much, Your Grace."

"Excellent. Lord and Lady Farren have just expressed a desire to take a turn around the rest of the gardens. I thought to join them if you will accompany me."

As he smiled down at her, Julia felt her heart catch a beat. At last! Here was her chance to have a few moments of privacy with him.

"I would enjoy a walk, Your Grace." She smiled into his eyes.

This time, she would take her courage well in hand. Surely, by his seeking her out like this so pointedly, it evidenced a certain regard for her. Her confidence grew at this thought.

With a thrill of excitement, Julia took the arm the duke offered and moved off with him to join Caro and Clive.

This time she would not let any missish fears inhibit her desire to beguile the duke.

Chapter Sixteen

*I*n the deepening twilight, the duke and Julia walked down the graveled path, with Clive and Caro trailing behind. Reaching a narrow stone bridge, they paused, watching a child throw flower petals into the water below. Like tiny rafts, the petals floated along the canal that cut through Sydney Gardens.

The festive glow from the colorful, paper-covered lanterns reflecting on the moving water added to the ambience of fantasy that filled the evening air. Glancing back, Julia smiled at the sight of Clive and Caro standing close together, gazing at each other passionately.

"What makes you smile, Miss Allard?" the duke asked quietly.

"My cousins," she replied simply.

The duke glanced back at the couple. "They are newly married, are they not?"

"Yes, almost seven months now."

"Obviously, their affection for each other is great. They are fortunate."

"Yes, they are indeed fortunate." At least Clive did not invite his mother to join them for their walk through the Gardens, she thought wryly.

By this time, a half a dozen people joined them on the bridge, their raucous laughter jarring the intimacy that had gently surrounded the duke and Julia.

"Shall we continue?"

Nodding her agreement to his suggestion, Julia turned and walked with him over the rest of the bridge, to another path lined with colorful lanterns.

In a short time, they left the boisterous little crowd behind. Soft night air silently enveloped them, and birds flying to roost for the night rustled the tree branches above them. Breathing deeply, the scent of night-blooming flowers assailed her senses.

Keenly conscious of the duke walking next to her, Julia said nothing. It was odd, but no tension filled the silence between them. The excitement that had been building within her all week suddenly faded away. No longer plagued by anxiety, an unexpected sense of calm came over her.

Glancing over her shoulder as they passed another couple, she noticed that they had left Caro and Clive somewhere behind. Pushing aside the possible consequences of her brazen actions, she kept walking with the duke.

From a distance, music filled the air as the orchestra began a rich concerto.

The blatant romance saturating the twilight touched Julia. Cutting a sideways glance up at the duke, she wondered how it would feel to be in this lovely setting with the man she loved.

They continued along the serpentine, shrubbery-lined path that led deeper into the interior of the park.

Without her realizing it, they had arrived at the ivy-covered stone alcove she and Caro had walked to on her first visit to the Gardens—the visit in which the duke had caught her unaware. The visit in which he had given her his insufferable excuse of an apology, she realized with a dull twinge of anger.

Because of the deep gloom, she could not see the picturesque spring she knew was nearby. But she could hear the sound of bubbling water. Though people were probably within ten yards of them, this sudden sense of privacy caused another shiver to travel up her arms.

She walked a few paces toward the alcove before realizing the duke had stopped nearer the overgrown hedge by the spring.

Turning, she was able to study him from a safe distance. He was at his ease, his weight shifted negligently on his left leg. The dim glow of a lantern hanging from a low, bent tree branch near him provided little light. There was barely enough illumination to reveal his features. He was gazing at her with that perceptive, slightly raffish grin she was coming to know so well.

Inhaling, she relished the luscious, heavy scent of jasmine. At the faint breeze skimming across her arms, she pulled her shawl a little higher around her shoulders and continued to gaze at the duke.

His expression, though relaxed, was alert as he moved to lean his shoulder against the tree. She sensed that he was waiting for her to speak.

A pleasurable shiver raced over her body. A night bird sang in concert with the distant melody of the orchestra.

"How lovely."

Something in the deep timbre of his voice made the words a compliment to her, instead of the music.

Struggling for a response, Julia wondered what it was about him that seemed to freeze the words in her throat.

Her eyes searched his face in the soft golden lamplit glow. What did she really know of this man? Firmly, she reminded herself that she knew all she need to know.

Suddenly, a sense of urgency gripped her. She wanted to get it over with—to have this desire for revenge exorcised. If she did not, she was convinced she would never feel like herself again.

Slowly, she approached. When she was within a couple of yards of him, he pushed himself from the tree.

"Yes, the music is lovely." The husky tone of her own voice surprised her.

She was close enough to see his lips quirk into a hint of a smile. "From our short acquaintance, I had not thought you to resort to coyness, Miss Allard. You know very well that I was not referring to the music."

Surprised by his bluntness, Julia could not prevent the mischievous smile from rising to her lips. "At the risk of being called coy again, I would say that it is the height of presumption to assume a seemingly general comment was meant to flatter me, Your Grace."

His rich laughter caused her smile to widen. "This is why I dislike complimenting a beautiful woman. She receives so many, any compliment must seem mundane."

"It depends on who is giving the compliment—and on the compliment itself. Flattery, no matter how prettily put, is indeed mundane. But a sincere compliment would always be appreciated."

He took a few steps closer to her. She did not retreat, and now there was less than a step between them.

"There are many kinds of compliments," he said softly.

"Are there?"

"Yes. For instance, the fact that you are with me now—after the insult I so foolishly handed you last year—is a great compliment."

The lightness of his tone caused her to lower her gaze from his. Oh, why had he brought up that kiss at this moment? His expression of regret divided her resolve. She now knew enough of his character to know that he was sorry for that day in London. But such was his innate arrogance that it was painfully apparent that he had never given any thought to what his actions may have cost her.

Choking back the words bursting from her heart, she raised her eyes back up to his.

"You have already apologized, Your Grace."

"You are a most extraordinary young lady, Miss Allard."

Unexpected warmth began to grow in the pit of her stomach as she watched his gaze settle on her mouth.

"And I think you are an extraordinary gentleman," she whispered.

As naturally as the setting of the sun, the space between them disappeared.

Finding herself suddenly in his arms, Julia felt a flash of panic. Every innate instinct told her to withdraw, to take care. But a wave of heat fogged her senses as she reminded herself of her desire for revenge. Relaxing, she did not resist the strength of his arms encircling her body.

His face was close to hers, and she no longer felt that she could pull her gaze from his. The strong outline of his jaw and the faint glitter of his gaze seemed to mesmerize her. Welcoming this strange— yet extremely pleasurable—sensation, she slowly moved her hands up his chest, until her arms were around his neck.

His arms tightened and she began to breathe fitfully. Feeling herself shiver in his embrace, she knew he was about to kiss her. As she waited, the warmth in the depths of her stomach spread through her limbs. This was nothing like that brief moment on Bolton Street. This was nothing like anything she had ever experienced.

"What is your given name?" His husky voice slipped over her senses, and she relaxed against him even more.

Closing her eyes against the depth of passion she saw in his, it took a moment to form the words. "Julia. And yours?"

A smile teased at the corner of his mouth, his head dipped lower. "Gryffen. 'Tis a family name from old, but I forbid you to use it. Call me Kel, Julia."

Gryffen. Julia. A faint alarm bell went off somewhere deep inside her befuddled senses. This whispered exchange of their names somehow felt even more intimate than the closeness of his embrace.

Gryffen. His name fit him. But the fact that he interrupted the magical moment to ask her name showed more sensitivity than she wanted to believe he possessed. This unexpected knowledge dulled the new, sensual feelings that had gripped her a moment ago.

Lifting her gaze to his, she looked at him in confusion. Doubt tried to surface through her churning emotions.

The words Caro had used to warn her suddenly came to mind—*"Have a care, while you are trying to make the duke lose his head, you may well lose yours."* Could this be what Caro had meant? This heady, heated feeling that befuddled her thoughts and took over her body?

Yet, the wholly unexpected warmth and awareness of having his muscular arms around her, with her breasts crushed against his chest, made her reluctant to break from his embrace.

The force of her unexpected reaction to him caused her another moment of panic. "I–I should not be here."

His arms tightened around her, and she saw a queer light enter his warm dark eyes.

"You are correct, my dear Julia," he said, lowering his head the last few inches that separated them.

Holding her breath, she held completely still. With her arms around his neck, she admitted to herself that despite her confusion, she was not going to pull away.

As his mouth descended to hers, she closed her eyes and lifted her lips to meet his. Thoughts of revenge flew far away as she melted into this new-found sensation of passion.

The warmth of his lips stayed on hers for only a moment, before moving to the corner of her mouth, then to her cheek. With infinite gentleness, his lips trailed up to her temple, then finally rested upon her forehead.

Feeling him pull back, she half opened her eyes to meet his glittering, passionate gaze.

"You are right, Julia, you should not be here."

Chapter Seventeen

*G*azing down into her silvery eyes, Kel allowed himself another moment to savor the feel of his arms around her slim torso before rebuking himself for this unexpected moment of poor judgment.

Although long experienced in recognizing the signs of passion in a woman's eyes, Miss Allard—Julia—was not a light skirt to be trifled with in this manner. Still, his gentlemanly intentions were at war with his body's instinctive response to the fire sparking in the smoky depths of her languid gaze. At this moment it was almost impossible to believe that he ever thought her cold.

Normally, he held himself, and his desires, in complete control. But here he was, in a place that afforded little privacy, with this stunning, mysterious woman in his arms.

Her behavior confused and intrigued him. His finely honed senses could not dismiss the feeling that she was concealing something from him. Except for that brief moment in the Orange Grove, when she had teased him about gambling in that adorably dry way, he did not believe that she had ever behaved naturally with him.

On the day he had apologized to her, she had

seemed frozen. At the time, he had put it down to the unexpectedness of his appearance. But during tea at the dowager Lady Farren's, he would have sworn that it was anger that had put a deep blush to her cheeks.

Then, at the ball, she had completely baffled him with her warm—even bold—glances and welcoming smile. His curiosity had been piqued, and he admitted to himself that Miss Julia Allard was beginning to fascinate him. Her natural grace and unaffected confidence was an alluring change from the overly refined London miss, or coquettish opera dancer he usually encountered.

It did not surprise him that he felt physical desire for her—he scarce knew a man who would not. But the desire to have a deeper knowledge of her character took him by surprise.

Instinctively, he felt she was playing some sort of game with him. When he asked her to take a stroll around the park this evening, her nervousness had been almost palpable. Yet, she now invited his kiss.

Feeling a strong temptation to kiss her properly, he decided that whatever the game, he was more than willing to enter into it.

Even as he held her, feeling as if he could lose his bearings in the beauty of her eyes, he was aware of the folly of indulging his desires. He reminded himself that someone could come upon them at any moment. He cared not a damn for himself, but it would not do to have Julia embarrassed.

No matter how inexplicable he found her behavior, it was his duty as a gentleman not to place her in a compromising situation, no matter how willing she seemed.

"We should return," he said softly.

Self-conscious confusion instantly clouded her gaze. "Yes."

When she pulled back slightly, he immediately released her. Taking a step back, she made a show of fussing with her shawl.

He smiled at her contradictory actions. A moment ago the light in her eyes promised a deep and pure passion that made him want to pull her back into his arms. Now he would swear that she was blushing.

"My dear Julia, I do not believe you know your own mind."

Again, a look that was not quite confusion, not quite anger flashed in her gaze. "Of course I do."

The note of forced bravado did little to convince him.

Not wanting to upset her further, he said nothing as they left the ivy-covered alcove. Stepping onto the path that led back to the little footbridge, he glanced at her face, revealed in the glow from the lanterns lining the path. "You are a very mysterious young lady."

The nervous tone beneath her brief laugh convinced him that he was correct in his assessment that she was concealing something from him.

"You would be surprised at how transparent I truly am—there is nothing at all mysterious about me. You just do not know me."

"Then we should remedy that."

She made no comment to this as they continued along the path, passing a few couples and small groups of people enjoying the fine spring evening.

"I am serious, Miss Allard. I am determined to solve the puzzle of you." He saw the quick, uneasy glance she sent him.

"That almost sounds like a warning." Her little laugh sounded forced.

"Not at all. A declaration. I take pleasure in solving mysteries."

"You are quite mistaken, Your Grace. As I said

before, there is no mystery about me. I am a simple, straightforward person."

"You may be a number of things, but I'd wager simple and straightforward are not among them."

She directed the full force of her shadowed gray gaze at him. "And if you solve this so-called mystery, what then?"

"I have the feeling another one would soon take its place."

He saw a quick flash of surprise cross her face, before she gave a dismissive shrug. "Why bother solving one mystery to just go on to another? That seems as if it would soon pall."

"It depends on the answer to the mystery. Some mysteries are endlessly fascinating."

In response, her steps quickened.

They had reached the footbridge, where several other people where enjoying the view. The congestion forced her to stop.

Leaning down slightly so no one else would hear, he asked, "Why suddenly so skittish?"

She turned to him, her eyes glinting with a spark of anger. "I have never been skittish a day in my life, Your Grace."

Her tart tone caused him to chuckle. "Forgive me, you may be correct. I have often been surprised at your lack of skittishness."

He smiled into her searching gaze. She was the first to look away.

"In truth, I have been surprising myself of late."

He caught the sigh in her words and frowned. Again, her enigmatic comment deepened the air of mystery about her.

They crossed the bridge and meandered up the path, through the pockets of crowds, back to the torch-encircled area.

"There you are!"

In unison, the duke and Julia turned to see Lord and Lady Farren converging onto the path. Lady Farren was looking at them with an avidly curious expression.

"We got separated from you in the crush on the bridge. I'm so glad we finally found you."

"Yes, Miss Allard and I wondered where you newlyweds had gone. Shall we join the others? I believe the fireworks will be starting soon."

Glancing down, he sent a reassuring smile to Julia. Her smile was tentative beneath the forced serenity of her expression as she preceded him to the grassy clearing. The Farrens followed beside her.

With his eyes on the alluring curve of her nape, he still felt the heat of her supple body pressed so intimately against his.

Taking a deep breath before he followed, he made sure the languid expression he wore like a mask was securely in place.

Chapter Eighteen

"Thank goodness Mama took to her room with a headache! I have been on tenterhooks to hear what happened when you went off with the duke last night," Mariah stated as she nimbly stepped over a puddle.

She had arrived at the Farrens' townhouse a short time earlier, with the suggestion that they walk to the North Parade. Julia had agreed with alacrity.

Earlier that morning, Caro had invited Julia to join her as she made calls and shopped, but Julia had declined. She wanted more than anything to speak to Mariah, and had a strong suspicion that her friend would arrive at the townhouse as soon as was polite.

Now, at Mariah's comment, Julia looked over at her in alarm. "You do not think anyone noticed, do you? We left with Caro and Clive and returned with them—I was praying we were not conspicuous."

"Not at all. But I know you. I could tell by the look on your face that something occurred. Tell me!"

"I don't know how," Julia said, lifting the hem of her twilight blue walking gown to avoid another puddle.

"What happened?" Mariah demanded, her voice rising slightly with her impatience.

Shaking her head at the memory of last night, Julia said, "I finally got up my nerve enough to flirt with him. I do not know what I was thinking—it all became so confusing. At first, I hoped that he would declare his desire for me so I could sneer and toss a cutting reply, leaving him to nurse his wounded pride."

Mariah slowed her steps, gazing at Julia with keen interest. "Oh, how daring! But what did you do?"

"Nothing," Julia said with a dejected sigh.

"Nothing? You went off with a notorious rake and nothing happened?" Mariah was clearly incredulous.

Slowing her steps as well, Julia spoke in a hesitant tone. "Well, almost nothing. He did kiss me, but not the way he did in London. This was unexpected and gentle. But before he kissed me, he asked me my given name."

Mariah came to a complete halt, both brows rising. "That is certainly not how I expected the duke to behave."

Julia nodded in dismal agreement. "I do not know what to think about what happened. He is not at all what I assumed him to be—blast him."

"As much as it pains me to admit, after meeting him last night he is not what I expected either. He is so dashing and attentive. He does not at all seem like a libertine—although I know he is. So what now? Are you abandoning your plan to seek revenge?"

"Oh, Mariah, I am so confused. I do not know what to do—everything seems so different now. Am I just to pretend nothing happened—that I have not been hurt? Should I just ignore my pride?"

"I sympathize with your plight," Mariah said as they turned onto Duke Street. "It is too bad we cannot duel for our honor like gentlemen. I have always wanted to learn to fence properly."

"I know. The wooden swords we played with as children just weren't the same."

"What are you going to do now?"

"I think I am going to avoid the duke and give myself time to think. This is much trickier business than I had thought it would be. I have the feeling that he knows what I'm doing and finds it amusing." She did not tell her friend that in the sober afternoon light, free of the twilight romance of last eve, she had the suspicion that she had a lucky escape last night.

There was a moment in the alcove when revenge had been far from her mind. When he had held her so closely, she had felt as if she were melting against him. She blushed now at the way she had shamelessly put her arms around his neck and leaned against his tall body.

When they had returned to join the other guests within the torch-lit circle, Julia refused to look at the duke. But during the noisy, colorful fireworks display, she had not been able to resist seeking him out. It had caused an odd, breathless feeling in her chest the instant her gaze clashed with his disturbingly intense eyes.

Shaking her head to free herself from the memory, she continued to walk with Mariah toward the North Parade. She had not been there before, and Caro had told her how popular a spot it was for walking and meeting friends. Caro also claimed a superb view of the River Avon could be gained from the walkway that edged the parade.

How different her life looked on this unexpectedly fine day, she mused. She had lived for twenty-four years, her life no more or less difficult than anyone else's—and suddenly, everything she knew of herself was now a mass of confused sensations.

They walked in silence for a while before Mariah said hesitantly, "Maybe Caro, being newly married, is wisest after all—it could be foolish to tamper with the affections of a man. Especially a man like the Duke of Kelbourne. I would hate to see you get hurt worse than you have been already."

Julia knew that Mariah was correct, yet, there had been something so unexpected, so startling about those brief moments by the alcove, the scene kept repeating over and over in her mind.

They arrived at the graveled walkway that bordered the vast lawn of the North Parade, where it seemed half the citizens of Bath were congregating or promenading.

"Come, Mariah, let us put my foolishness aside and enjoy this beautiful afternoon." She could not face discussing the duke any further.

"You are never foolish, but I will not quiz you anymore about the dreadful duke." Mariah's smile showed gentle understanding.

They had not been strolling on the parade for very long, when Julia espied Caro and Clive standing with several other people. The duke was among them.

Mariah had seen them as well. "We cannot pretend we do not see them."

Feeling her heart instantly skip a beat, then begin to gallop, Julia swallowed and nodded. "No, I suppose not."

Slowly, they approached the group. Julia saw that besides the duke, Caro, and Clive, there was also the duke's sister, Lady Fallbrook, and his friend, Lord Mattonly. Clive and Lord Mattonly seemed to be engaged in an animated conversation.

Julia and Mariah were almost upon the little group when Caro turned and saw them. A welcoming smile spread across her face.

"Look who has joined us!" she announced with pleasure as Julia and Mariah made their curtsies. "You are just in time; we have been having a very lively discussion on one of your pet subjects, Julia." She turned back to Clive. "My dear husband, you will have no luck with our Julia if you broach this topic with her. *She* believes everyone who has the desire should learn to read. She is always teaching some youngster how to write his name and make out his letters."

Unable to look at the duke, Julia sent a smile to Lady Fallbrook and Lord Mattonly. However, before any greetings could be exchanged, Lord Farren turned his gimlet gaze to Julia.

"That so? Not wise, dear cousin. Before you know it, we shall have the lower orders thinking themselves ladies and gentlemen because they can read. Not wise at all."

Although quite relieved that she was saved from having to look at the duke for the moment, she was taken aback by this unexpected pronouncement.

Shrugging lightly, she said, "We shall have to disagree on this matter. Miss Thorncroft and I have helped some of the young people in our village learn to read. John Willingham, who came to us a few years ago, now has a good position at the local mercantile because he can write down orders. His employer is very pleased with him."

Everyone was attending her, but Julia was most keenly aware of the duke's eyes upon her. After casting him a quick glance, she lifted her chin in defiance at his surprised expression. She did not give a fig if he thought badly of her for her views, she thought with a hint of disappointment.

The others shifted their interested gazes to Lord Farren, waiting for his rebuttal. He cleared his voice once or twice before replying.

"Well," Clive began in a doubtful tone, "I'm sure there are exceptions, but all in all it's bad business teaching the masses to read. However, I expect a sheltered young lady like you would not be able to see the larger ramifications. Eh, what, Your Grace?" he stated, looking to the duke to confirm this wisdom.

The duke, who had been leaning casually on his

silver-handled walking stick, shifted his weight before answering. "I happen to concur with Miss Allard on this subject, Farren. I have always believed, as did my father, that to be able to read is important, at whatever station in life people find themselves. A man who reads is a better worker, for one thing. Moreover, to be able to read edifying material for oneself can only add to the sense of personal dignity."

"Indeed, my brother has always supported and promoted education in his village," Lady Fallbrook put in with a proud smile directed toward her brother.

Julia stared up at the duke, flummoxed that he held an opinion so near to her own on such a controversial subject. It was the last thing she expected to hear him say, and she did not know what to do with this information.

Although she was prepared to admit to herself that she did not think as badly of the duke as she had before last night, this new knowledge did not meld with her opinion of him as completely selfish.

"You certainly have a point, Your Grace. I shall be giving the matter some more thought," Clive stated, attempting to retreat from his previous stance with some dignity.

Julia continued to look at the duke, her luminous gray eyes revealing more of her confusion than she would have liked.

"Well, now that we have had a good dose of intellectual conversation, shall we take a turn along the river's edge?"

It was apparent that Lady Fallbrook's question was meant for the group, and with general agreement, they all turned toward the River Avon. After sending Julia what could only be interpreted as an encouraging smile, Mariah moved to Caro's side.

A gentle breeze whipped frothy caps on the choppy waves, and although Julia kept her eyes on the river, she was aware that the duke had moved to her side.

Julia was also aware that the others were already a few steps ahead, but she made no move to catch up. She felt the heat of a blush rise to her cheeks as she recalled how close he held her last eve.

"I confess, Miss Allard, your opinion on the subject of education surprises me. I thought fashionable young ladies occupied themselves with the pianoforte and needlework." His laconic tone held a hint of amusement.

"And I thought dukes only occupied themselves with gambling and the fit of their coats." The smile she sent him belied her arch tone.

"Perhaps we both are wrong in certain assumptions we hold."

Something in the seriousness of his deep voice stilled her smile, and she found it difficult to pull her gaze from his dark eyes.

"Mayhap," she found herself whispering back.

A jolt of instinctive panic shot through her body. This would not do! She could not let one, and surely lone, positive attribute color what she knew to be true. Just because he agreed with her on a subject dear to her heart did not detract from how dissolute and immoral she knew him to be. No, this one good aspect of his character could not change her opinion. Yet, alarm fluttered through her heart, for she suddenly realized that she was finding it increasingly difficult to hold on to her hatred of him.

This would not do, she thought again, giving herself a mental shake. She reminded herself that he was everything she disliked in a man—arrogant, insufferable, and selfish.

Pulling her gaze from his, she struggled for a light tone. "I must confess that you have found me out, Your Grace. I care for little else but playing the pianoforte, and I enjoy the more artistic aspects of embroidery." She hoped this would dispel the sudden feeling of intimacy that had tethered her to him in the last few minutes.

Cutting a sideways glance, she saw his dark brows draw together as he sent her a slanting glance.

"Doing it a bit too brown, Miss Allard. A little late in the day to try to appear the shallow miss. I know better. Although, I have no idea why you would desire to give me a distorted impression of your character."

"I do not believe I have made any effort to give you an impression of my character, distorted or otherwise."

"Whether or not you have made an effort, in our short acquaintance, I have come to have a better understanding of your temperament."

"Indeed?" Julia lifted her chin to a haughty tilt. "You must be finding Bath exceedingly dull to make a study of me, Your Grace."

As hard as she tried to prevent it, his rich laughter caused an answering smile to come to her lips.

"Yes, Bath is rather dull, but that does not mean I have been bored."

"I own you have not seemed bored, just rather amused by all of us mortals."

"To find amusement in the folly of life is a trait, or maybe fault, that I readily admit. But well you know that last night I was not amused—and you should be aware of how very mortal I am."

Swiftly, her gaze went to his. They were several yards behind the others, and Julia was glad of it. Heat flew to her cheeks, even though she thought that she was past blushing where the duke was concerned.

Once again, a mortifying loss of words gripped her as she met his intense, solemn gaze.

At this moment nothing about him seemed amused or glib, although she did sense a certain air of watchfulness beneath his calm, confident demeanor.

Pulling her troubled gaze from his, she trained her eyes on the grassy embankment of the River Avon. The fact that he was so straightforward about what happened last night did something strange to her heart.

They had caught up to the others, who had stopped to watch some swans feeding on the river.

"They are so lovely," Julia said in an attempt to change the subject.

"Yes, they are. I have swans on my lake at Kelbourne Keep. They are interesting creatures in the fact that they mate for life."

Her eyes swiftly went to his dark gaze. The breath caught in her throat at the unexpected expression she met. Forcing a sophisticated little laugh, she said, "You almost sound as if you find fidelity an admirable quality—in swans."

"Your Grace, my husband and I are so pleased that you are to be joining us for our dinner party this Friday."

Caro's cheerful voice cut through before the duke could respond. The spell that seemed to hold Julia's gaze to the duke's broke. Releasing the breath she had not realized she was holding, Julia forced herself to look to her cousin.

" 'Pon my word, Lady Farren, I am pleased as well," the duke pronounced.

Julia immediately noticed that the languid amusement had returned to his tone. It also occurred to her that he never used that particular tone when he was speaking only to her.

So much for her plan to avoid the duke so that she could think, Julia thought with dismay.

Chapter Nineteen

*J*ulia spent the day of Caro's party writing a reply to the letter she had received that morning from her aunt Beryl. With quill hovering over the piece of foolscap, Julia felt torn between disappointment and relief that Uncle John and Aunt Beryl would not be coming to Bath as previously planned.

Part of her wanted to pour out her confusion and doubt onto her aunt's loving shoulder—as she had always done.

The other part of her, the part that was full of lingering resentment and vengeful schemes, knew that her aunt and uncle would insist she return to Chippenham if they had a hint of her behavior with the duke. The knowledge that they would be terribly disappointed if they knew she had wandered off with the duke in Sydney Gardens caused a hot blush to rise to her cheeks.

With some difficulty, she put her attention back to the letter and wrote a few more lines.

The black clouds that had been rolling into Bath all day had not helped her mood. Normally, she enjoyed a ripping storm. However, today the booming waves of distant thunder set her nerves on edge. As the thrumming sound grew heavier and nearer, the flashes of lightning made her tense and uneasy.

At the sound of the door opening, Julia turned curiously to see a harried-looking Caro rush into the room.

"I could scream. Do you know what my mama-in-law has done now?" Caro asked without preamble.

With a curious frown, Julia set aside her letter as Caro flopped dejectedly into the chair by the window.

"What has she done to put you in such a pet?"

"Tonight, Clive and I are giving our first large party. Not five minutes ago, Hill brought me a letter from her. It is a list of items she deems need my attention before our guests arrive."

"Such as?" Julia asked a little doubtfully, for she did not think this seemed such a grievous insult.

"She suggests that I make sure the servants polish the silver! She suggests that new candles be placed in the sconces and chandeliers so they will not sputter! As if my own mother did not teach me the proper way to run a household! I have a good mind to send her a note telling her just what I think of her silly list."

With a sympathetic smile, Julia said, "Pay her no mind, she is just trying to goad you. It has not escaped her notice that Clive is not as quick to jump when she calls. Actually, you should be pleased; this shows you are winning."

The anxious expression on Caro's brow lightened considerably. "Clive has certainly been more attentive lately. However, I am not going to relax too quickly, he could relapse. Still, my mother-in-law infuriates me with her insinuations that I am not a good housekeeper or hostess."

"It could be that her servants are so ill-trained that she has to worry about such things," Julia said with a mischievous smile. "But you are much too competent, and your home is too well run to worry about such trifles."

Caro clapped her hands. "I like that. I shall just ignore her. I can afford to be magnanimous this week. But now that I have calmed down, I can see that I have interrupted your letter writing."

"It matters not," Julia said. "I was just writing to Aunt Beryl. I am sure you have already received her regrets for your party. Uncle John is still recovering from his head cold. I am disappointed, I have never been so long without their company."

"I am disappointed for another reason," Caro replied. "I was hoping the presence of our aunt and uncle would dissuade you from continuing to make sheep's eyes at the duke."

Julia's expression showed her complete shock at these words.

"Sheep's eyes! I have never been so inelegant as to make sheep's eyes at anyone."

"I may have put it a bit too strongly. But you did give him all of your attention yesterday. I cannot say that I blame you. I was probably batting my lashes at him as well. The way he so courteously listened to me and looked into my eyes . . ." Her voice trailed off on a sigh. " 'Tis hard to dismiss so much amiability and ease of manner in one so grand."

Julia said nothing. As much as she resisted the thought, a part of her acknowledged the truth of Caro's words. The duke was startlingly charming.

"You must admit, Julia, the duke is not the boor you thought him to be."

Julia fiddled with her quill. "He is not all bad—people rarely are. But his pleasing ways cannot change the fact that he is selfish and arrogant."

Caro sighed. "Cannot you see that you are placing your reputation in further danger? If your good name was in question before, what do you think will be said

if you continue in this foolish manner? Not that there
has been any gossip about you in Bath—but that can
easily change if you are not a little more careful."

Julia looked into her cousin's concerned gaze for a
moment before coming to a decision. "A-actually I
am not at all sure how I shall proceed where the
duke is concerned."

Caro's brows rose in surprise. "I will thank all the
saints if you are finally seeing reason."

Several hours later, as the rain pounded the hills
of Bath, Julia was beginning to believe she would
soon pace a hole in the rug on the floor of her pretty
bedchamber. A clap of thunder caused her to give a
nervous start as she walked past the fireplace for the
twentieth time.

Earlier, she had sent a servant over to Mariah's
hotel, asking her to come to the townhouse a little
before the party started.

After a few more minutes of impatient pacing, she
heard a tap at the door. Practically running across
the room, Julia pulled the door open and was enormously pleased to see Mariah, who was dressed in
a sapphire blue evening gown.

"Thank you for coming early," Julia said, pulling
her into the room and shutting the door.

"Not at all, I was intending to arrive before Caro's
party started, anyway. Mama wanted to come early
so that she can evaluate the unattached young men
as they arrive. Besides, I wanted to speak to you as
well—I have been concerned about you."

Waving her hand, Julia directed her friend to be
seated on the vanity chair, before sitting on the bed.
"In what way?"

"Seeing you and the duke together yesterday
changed my whole opinion on this revenge business.
I now believe that you should stop right now."

The note of deep concern in Mariah's voice could not be ignored.

"What about seeing me and the duke together has brought you to this opinion?"

"While watching him with you at the river, I had the feeling that he has been through these kinds of sophisticated flirtations a thousand times. He is a hundred steps ahead of you. He is so attractive and polished, he is dangerous. More dangerous now that you no longer hate him. Do not bother to deny it, I saw it on your face yesterday."

"I won't," Julia said quietly, smoothing the front of her rose pink gown with nervous fingers. "Too much has happened too quickly. My mind is spinning with so many conflicting thoughts about the duke. Why couldn't things have stayed simple? It was much easier to hate him when all I knew of him was that he kissed unsuspecting women on the street for a lark. I cannot forgive him, yet I no longer hate him. I certainly find myself at a pretty pass."

An empty feeling settled in the pit of her stomach as she continued, "You are right. I am finished with this nonsense. I shall return home in a few weeks, pick up the threads of my old life, and never think of him again. No need to worry that I shall make myself ridiculous where the duke is concerned."

"I was never worried about that, m'dear. But I confess that I am relieved that you have given up this notion of revenge, even though I was dreadful in the way I encouraged you."

"Never say so—you have been a wonderful friend! I am so glad you are here. For some reason, all day I have been as skittish as a cat near the kennels." Rising from the bed, Julia forced a smile in an attempt to make light of her nervousness.

Smiling, Mariah stood up as well. "You cannot be worse than my mama has been this evening. Since the gala night, she is convinced that because of this new connection with the duke and his family, a titled gentleman will suddenly fall in love at the sight of me. She is determined to see me in a coronet if she has to send Papa to debtors' prison to do it. Shall we go down so that I may be put on display?"

"Yes, I think we may be late enough to make a grand entrance," Julia said, picking up her shell pink shawl from the foot of the bed. A moment later they left the room, arm in arm.

An hour and a half later, Julia and Mariah were standing in the main salon, near the double doors that led to the dining room. Footmen moved discreetly among the guests, replacing empty wineglasses with full ones. There was a pleasant hum of conversation, occasionally interspersed with laughter.

Despite the convivial atmosphere, Julia felt as uneasy as she had earlier.

The duke's arrival had only heightened her anxiety. Now she congratulated herself, for after their initial greeting she had hardly looked in his direction.

She had to confess that it was almost impossible to ignore him, such was his air of consequence and imposing physical presence. It was as if she were trying to pretend that a lion was not prowling the room.

"Despite the dowager Lady Farren's unsubtle hints, I must say that Caro is on her mettle this evening. Everyone seems more than pleased," Mariah stated, recalling Julia's attention.

"I agree." Julia had shared with her friend the contents of the dowager's insulting note. In response, both young ladies had done their best to be as engaging and amiable as they could to help ensure the success of the evening.

Catching Caro's eye, Julia sent an encouraging smile to her cousin. Gracefully breaking away from her conversation with the elderly Colonel Asher—a charmer Julia had met earlier—Caro crossed the room to join Julia and Mariah.

"Do you think it is going well—does everyone seem to be happy?" Caro's tone revealed how concerned she was despite her façade of confidence.

"It has turned into a lovely evening, Caro. You are doing a beautiful job," Julia said.

"I am just pleased that all this thunder and lightning has not prevented anyone on my guest list from coming this evening. As long as all is well in the kitchen, I shall breathe easy."

"I would not worry about a thing, Caro. It is a wonderful party. The rain beating on the windowpanes has only made us all feel cozy. On a night like this, everyone feels obliged to be pleasant," Mariah offered in the tone of a sage.

"They do? Why?" Caro asked curiously.

"Well, 'tis more desirable to be at a lovely gathering than to give into the bad weather and go to bed with a fit of the doldrums."

Julia and Caro laughed at Mariah's bit of whimsy.

"As I am feeling quite obliged to be pleasant, I shall be a good guest and go and converse with some of the others," Julia told them.

She had espied Mr. Dillingham on the other side of the room with Lady Davinia and the dowager Lady Farren. Julia had not seen him since the evening of the latter lady's ball.

A twinge of guilt tugged at her conscience, for she had not given Mr. Dillingham or their budding relationship a thought since the dowager Lady Farren's ball.

As she moved across the room, she made sure to give the duke a wide berth. How effortlessly he commanded attention, she noticed, her eyes on his strong profile. With the other guests standing around him, it was as if he stood in the eye of a colorful, chattering storm. It surprised her a little to see that he was not wearing his usual bored expression.

At that moment the duke turned, and above the heads of those around him, his dark penetrating gaze met hers.

For an instant, she felt as if one of the flashes of lightning raging outside sparked between them, leaving her breathless and shocked.

Quickly looking away, she continued to cross the room, feeling slightly dazed.

No matter how she tried, the memory of being in his arms could not be dismissed. She had been completely unprepared for the feelings the intimate encounter had created.

It was not just the unexpected sense of melting passion that stayed with her. It was the duke's gentleness—mixed with unmistakable desire—that continued to reverberate within her.

The intimate look that just passed between them reminded her of the way he had asked her name before kissing her so gently.

A shiver feathered across the back of her neck and down her spine.

The deep intensity of his whispered question stayed with her like a haunting dream. Odd that such a simple thing could affect her so acutely.

Continuing to cross the room, she suddenly realized that if the duke had not stopped, she would have stayed in his arms without giving a care to the ramifications.

What a widgeon I was to think that I could ever best a man like the duke in games of the heart, she chided herself. But she wondered again why he had been the first to put an end to their embrace.

Another muffled clap of thunder pulled her from these disturbing thoughts.

As she moved toward Mr. Dillingham and Lady Davinia, she was aware of the heavy, empty feeling settling in the pit of her stomach.

Sensing her presence, Lady Davinia turned and smiled. "Dear Miss Allard, how lovely to see you again. I confess I have been hoping to meet you again since our encounter at the Orange Grove." Lady Davinia's expression and tone of voice leant sincerity to her words.

"You are too kind, Lady Davinia." Julia smiled, curtsied, and greeted the dowager and Mr. Dillingham.

"Good evening, Miss Allard. I was just saying to Lady Farren and Lady Davinia that the last time I had such a pleasant evening was at Lady Farren's wonderful ball."

"I certainly agree with you, Mr. Dillingham," Julia said.

"I daresay that I would not be flattering myself to say that my daughter-in-law has learned a bit about entertaining from me," Lady Farren said, preening shamelessly.

Keeping the smile pasted to her face, Julia decided that it was the better part of valor—and being a good guest—to let this remark pass without comment.

To her relief, a moment later another guest drew the dowager away.

"Miss Allard, I am determined to get to know you better. Do tell me about yourself," Lady Davinia beseeched.

With a surprised laugh, Julia said, "There is very little to tell."

Lady Davinia started to reply when the large double doors opened, and Hill, the butler, stepped in.

Three gentlemen passed him in a desultory fashion and strode into the room.

All conversation stopped as everyone turned to see who had arrived.

"My lord Haverstone, my lord Alton, and Mr. Morton," Hill announced into the sudden silence.

Curiously, Julia looked over at the group. All the men were dressed in expertly tailored evening clothes of the finest material.

The first gentleman took a few more steps into the room and halted. Julia assumed he was Lord Haverstone, as he was the first to be announced. With his weight on one leg in an elegantly negligent fashion, he pulled a quizzing glass as his friends moved to flank him.

With an impressive lack of self-consciousness, Lord Alton raised the glass to his eye and began to leisurely scan the room.

A little distance away, Julia saw Mrs. Thorncroft scurry up behind Mariah. "Posture, Mariah, posture," she whispered, giving her daughter a swift poke between the shoulder blades.

Turning her gaze back to the gentlemen, Julia felt the anxiousness that had been plaguing her all day swell up and choke her.

"'Pon my soul, there you are, Kel!" Lord Haverstone said as his gaze came to rest on the duke. "See, Alton, Morton? We have finally run him to ground."

"Jolly good! Must say Bath is the last place I would have looked," said Lord Alton.

"Bath *is* the last place we looked, Alton," the third gentleman informed him in a dry tone.

Julia took a gulp of air as the men continued to gaze around the room, their expressions conveying a combination of curiosity and haughtiness.

From the corner of her eye, Julia saw the duke, who had been on the opposite end of the room when the men had entered, begin to move toward them.

Clive was closer and overcame his surprise enough to step forward, arms wide in welcome. "My lords, Mr. Morton! How very good of you to come. When we met earlier, I confess that I did not entertain the hope that you would accept my invitation. Welcome, welcome!" He turned and made a quick gesture to one of the footmen. "May I offer you a glass of wine?"

Julia watched in growing alarm as Clive continued to make the newcomers welcome. An instant later, Caro hurried forward, her face wreathed in a smile of delighted welcome.

Maybe her earlier fit of nerves had been some sort of premonition, Julia thought, for although she felt alarmed, she was not truly surprised to see these three men.

Always in the back of her mind, since meeting Lord Mattonly, was the possibility that the duke's other friends might turn up as well. As the days had passed, she had grown less worried, but the niggling fear had not gone completely away.

Now, standing beneath the ornate, crystal chandelier, her fingers reflexively gripped the handle of her ivory fan. White flashes of lightning, coming through the half-closed drapery knifed through the room's warm, candlelit glow.

Her gaze stayed on the three elegant men as Clive and Caro fluttered around them, looking excessively pleased. As if in slow motion, Julia watched the duke making his way through the clusters of guests.

Although some of the guests had resumed their conversations, the noise level was not what it had been a few moments ago.

Almost absentmindedly, Julia took note of Lord Alton. The tallest of the three, he was handsome despite his harsh features. His raven hair and blue eyes seemed to confirm the coldness she sensed from him.

He was only half paying attention to his hosts as Julia watched him raise the quizzing glass to his left eye. He resumed his casual perusal of the other guests, heedless that a number of them stared back.

Another flash sliced across the salon, and Julia saw the lightning flicker eerily off Lord Haverstone's quizzing glass. A rumble of thunder shortly followed.

An instant later, her gaze met his light blue eyes for a brief moment, and then his gaze moved on. Julia held her breath as she saw Lord Haverstone's body still before he swung his gaze back to her.

He stared for a moment and then swept her figure with keen regard. Lowering his glass, he turned to his friends. "Egad," he drawled, "Kel, do confess that this is the gel that you kissed on Bolton Street last year. No wonder we could never find her—she's been in Bath, of all godforsaken places."

Julia's breathing froze. If the room had not been so unnaturally quiet because of their unexpected arrival, she was sure that no one but the duke would have heard this comment. But by their shocked expressions, it was apparent to her that Lady Davinia and Mr. Dillingham must have heard Lord Haverstone's words.

Taking a very deep breath, Julia felt oddly detached from her surroundings. She only felt a stab of regret that Caro's lovely party was about to be thoroughly ruined.

Seemingly oblivious to the other guests, Mr. Morton stepped forward and squinted at Julia for a moment. Glancing over his shoulder, he tossed the duke a grin. "Kel, you sly dog! We've been scratchin' our noggins as to why you would choose to rusticate in Bath. Well, well, well! Now we know why."

Sparing a brief glance to the duke, Julia saw the

thunderous frown come to his brow, before she looked at Caro. Her cousin's expression was deeply pained, and Clive and his mama looked thunderstruck.

The duke stepped forward, and Julia felt an immediate and overwhelming need to escape.

She could feel everyone's eyes upon her as she quickly looked around for the quickest way of leaving the room.

The duke and his odious friends were between her and the double doors that opened to the hall, which led to the staircase.

Her only other choice was to go into the dining room, which had a door that led into the kitchen and French doors that opened to the back garden.

Refusing to so much as glance in the duke's direction, Julia lifted her chin in unconscious defiance. In a last desperate attempt to salvage a shred of her dignity, she struggled for an air of naturalness and grace as she swept into a deep curtsy.

"Please excuse me," she said, rising as smoothly as she could.

Fighting the urge to run, she moved past a number of guests, opened one of the dining room doors, stepped into the room, and closed it behind her, leaving the gaping faces behind.

Several servants, in the midst of putting the final touches to the gorgeous dining table, looked up in shock, for dinner would not be served for another fifteen minutes.

Without uttering a word, Julia walked the length of the table to the French doors. Wincing at a flash of lightning, she opened the door and stepped into the storm-swept garden.

Chapter Twenty

Within seconds of stepping into the garden, Julia was soaked. Squinting into the driving rain, she looked around for a place to shelter.

Instantly, she recalled the folly in the far corner of the garden. It was built in the style of a miniature Roman ruin, with four columns and an open work lattice roof with trailing vines. Gathering handfuls of her sodden gown, she lifted it enough so that she could run across the lawn with ease.

By the time she reached the folly, her slippers were oozing with mud and her gown clung to her in heavy wet folds.

Leaning against one of the stone pillars, she looked up at the vine-covered lattice that acted as the roof. It afforded little protection from the downpour, but she did not care. Staying one more second in the salon was an intolerable thought.

Pushing away from the pillar, she wrapped her arms around her waist and moved to the bench. Sitting down on the cold stone, she looked back toward the townhouse. The draperies were open on the long windows on either side of the French doors. The light spilling from the windows and the full moon glowing through the rolling clouds, kept her haven from being enveloped in darkness.

Good heavens! What had she just done? Raising her cold wet fingers to her cheeks, she could not prevent a horrified laugh. What a shocking mess she had left Caro to deal with.

Leaving was better than staying to endure more of the duke's friends' cutting comments, she thought angrily.

However, there was no escaping the truth that this was truly a dreadful situation. It was bad enough to have people whispering about her in Chippenham— at least no one had known exactly what had occurred in London. But now . . . she shook her head in despair.

"Now what?" she said aloud, lowering her hands to her lap.

"You took the words out of my mouth."

At the sound of his deep voice, Julia jumped up to stare at the duke in utter shock. Even the thunder suspended its fury for a moment.

The rain had plastered down his hair, and his cravat hung in damp folds. The brooding concern so obviously etched on his face gave her a moment's pause.

"Julia, please allow me to apologize for my friend's crass behavior. I know this must be embarrassing . . ."

"Embarrassing? Do you think I care?" she said, well aware of the ring of false bravado in her tone. The look of surprised confusion on his face gave her a brief flicker of satisfaction. "I am beyond being embarrassed by what you did that day in London, Your Grace." She pushed a wet strand of hair off her cheek with a quick, angry gesture.

He moved away from the pillar and took a stride closer. "I can understand your anger . . ."

Her harsh laugh coincided with a flash of lightning. The patter of raindrops grew louder on the stone floor.

"I am all astonishment at how understanding you are. It is rather amusing really—just when I decided to quit this game, your boorish friends arrive," she said with a bemused shake of her head before continuing. "Please spare me your understanding."

He stood before her in silence. Another crack of thunder illuminated the garden, and for a split second, his frowning, chiseled features were revealed in stark detail.

"You decided to quit this game," he repeated, his voice had the beginnings of a slight edge. "So the truth is finally beginning to surface. I confess you have held my interest with your so-called game. It has been amusing to guess what you will do next— one day you seem as if you wish to challenge me to fisticuffs, the next you are willingly in my arms."

"Oh, that? Heavens, that was just a lark. You know all about larks, don't you, Your Grace?"

Her breath caught as she strained to see his face. Finally the words were out, and she hoped they had drawn blood.

Clenching her rain-damp hands to her sides, she waited for his reaction. Watching him closely, she saw his eyes narrow slightly as he shifted his weight so that his legs were braced shoulder width apart.

"So that's the way of it. You *have* been playing a very cool game. I am curious as to what happened to change your mind since our regrettably innocent kiss at Sydney Gardens. Or did you just lose your nerve?"

Julia took note of the sarcastic emphasis he had put on the words "regrettably innocent." With a searing flash, her ire rose anew. "No, just my interest."

Her anger was even more piercing because his words rang true. She *had* lost her nerve, but not the way he meant. With a clarity that shamed her, she realized that her courage to exact revenge failed her because she had been foolish enough to become attracted to him.

As the rain continued to beat down upon them through the inadequate lattice roof, she realized that she did not feel the least bit of satisfaction at having lashed out at him.

Gazing up at his face in the clouded moonlight, she saw the barely concealed anger beneath his polished surface. "Congratulations, Julia. I would never have wagered that a green girl from the likes of Chippenham could have bested me in this kind of game." His amused drawl was in stark contrast to the cold look in his eyes.

A deep chill settled in her heart as well as her body. Staring up at him, she was aware that she felt more defeated than triumphant.

"You are truly amazing. Your arrogance is so all encompassing that you cannot see what your actions have wrought. Foolish of me to expect more from an unmitigated rakehell." Anger and disappointment joined the chill in her heart.

His next step brought him within inches of her, but Julia held her ground.

"What of you? Do you think nothing has come of your actions?"

"Of course. I should have stayed well clear of you. If I had, I would not be the object of scandalous speculation at this moment."

His broad shoulders lifted in a dismissive shrug. "You put too much store in the power of gossip. The opinion of a few inconsequentials in Bath matters little."

"How very easy for you to say. You set the rules in your world. In mine, I must follow the dictates of Society or suffer the consequences."

"Indeed? Have you been following these dictates while you have been in Bath?"

At his smooth perceptive tone, she looked away. She was glad for the relative darkness, for she felt the heat of a blush coming to her cheeks.

"No," she finally admitted reluctantly.

"Is it not more fun this way?"

Her gaze flew back up to his face at the gentle amusement that now laced his voice. Blast him! She would rather have died at that moment than to admit that he was right. Even if her behavior had not been so very shocking, she had found it exhilarating to flout propriety. And he knew it.

"I am sure it is fun for you, but not for those you leave in your wake." Sparing a second, she wondered why she felt sad instead of angry.

Rivulets of icy water ran down her neck and between her shoulder blades. Now the thunder and lightning flashed and cracked almost simultaneously as unseen black clouds virtually obliterated the moon glow.

The dim light from the dining room windows revealed him only in a shadowed outline. His nearness was causing very strange things to happen to her breathing. Why had he followed her? Why did he not go away? The feeling of being on the verge of losing control gripped her in a tangle of confusion.

"Our acquaintance has been amusing while it has lasted, Miss Allard. But I would hate for it to end with your opinion of me ruined." The sarcasm dripped from his words.

As he stepped closer, a tingling physical response shot through her body.

He was going to kiss her again, she realized instantly. As his arms went around her rain-soaked body, she did not resist. She was only aware of the same feeling that had come over her as she had stood alone with him in the alcove at Sydney Gardens. Breathless at his nearness, she allowed her body to remain pliant as he lowered his face to hers.

The cool rain joined their warm lips in a sensual melding as almost unconsciously she pressed her body against his. Her resentment and confusion joined with this new, nameless emotion. Why did she want to kiss him when she also felt like slapping him? These hazy thoughts faded into a swirl of passionate sensations as his arms tightened around her.

Almost before it began, the searing ardor of his kiss was cut short as he released her and stepped away.

She could barely make out his features as she swayed before him, feeling suddenly bereft and bewildered.

He spoke, but it took her a moment to comprehend his harshly whispered words.

"I may be a rakehell, but you, my dear Julia, are a hypocrite."

And then he was gone.

Chapter Twenty-one

"*L*ud, Julia, I wish you could have seen the look on the faces of Caro's guests! If I had not been so worried about you, I would have laughed." At Julia's pained expression, Mariah hastened to add, "How terribly mean of me. Of course it's not a laughing matter."

"Not to worry, I have somehow managed to find the humor in the situation," Julia said in a flat voice.

Lying on the damask-covered chaise in the sitting room adjacent to Caro's bedroom, Julia continued to sip her tea. She had not touched the little sandwiches on the tiered tray, nor had she eaten very much since Caro's ill-fated party two nights ago.

Seeing Caro and Mariah, seated across from her on a pretty settee exchanging a look of concern, Julia tried to rally her usual good spirits. Her efforts met with little success.

"I must say, Mariah, your mama was ever so helpful after Julia made her precipitous exit," Caro stated.

"I was quite surprised myself," Mariah replied, reaching for another watercress sandwich. "After the duke followed Julia from the room, everyone just stood there, dumbstruck. Suddenly, Mama spoke up and asked Lord Haverstone if he had any news of

London and Princess Charlotte's impending nuptials. She spoke in a perfectly normal tone, and I wondered how on earth she managed it."

Julia smiled faintly as Mariah continued her observations.

"It was rather astounding to watch you sweep out of the room, Julia. Everyone was completely confused, because no one else had heard what Lord Haverstone said. I do give you much credit for holding your chin high and not rushing. Then the duke said something to his friends before going out as well. But Mama kept chattering away in a perfectly droll manner until the butler announced dinner."

Nodding, Caro set her cup and saucer down. "I was so grateful to have those few moments to gain my composure. Dinner was quite odd. Everyone began to chatter, but no one referred to Julia or the duke—not even his friends."

"I am so sorry, Caro, I hope you can forgive me. I know how much the party meant to you," Julia said. The shadows beneath her gray eyes were evidence of the stress she felt.

"My dear Julia, I believe I would have done the same thing. Besides, everyone had a marvelous time. People love to have something to gossip about firsthand."

At that moment there was a knock at the door. Caro's lady's maid entered and handed her mistress a folded piece of paper.

After perusing the note, Caro rose with a look of chagrin. "Excuse me for a few moments, I must have a word with Cook."

After the door closed, Julia gazed at her friend, feeling inexplicably and utterly sad.

"I find myself in an impossible situation," Julia told Mariah quietly.

"Sadly, I must agree with you. I confess that I am

shocked that the duke is still in Bath. I saw him driving with his sister yesterday. His friends—how shockingly arrogant they are—swagger around town looking bored and superior. Why don't they go to London or Brighton? They are as out of place here as a monkey in church."

Despite the pain throbbing in her heart, Julia laughed at her friend's analogy.

"Only you could make such a comment at a time like this. I do wish I could just go home. But I have no hope of it, for with Uncle John feeling better, he and Aunt Beryl have decided to resume their trip to Bath."

"I thought you missed them."

"I do! But I want to go home—not have them come here! The last thing I wish to do is try to explain to them what has occurred since coming here. It is going to be unbearable because Aunt Beryl says she shall not be content until she has danced. So we are all to go to the Upper Rooms on Thursday."

"I would not be too concerned. The duke has not made an appearance at the Upper Rooms since coming to town."

"I am not really concerned about the duke. All the people who were at Caro's party cause me to shake in my slippers. This is dreadful. My aunt and uncle have been nothing but loving and supportive. I know how the gossip about me hurt them. It will be so much worse now that there is something solid for people to gossip about."

"Yes, it is all quite shocking. But your aunt and uncle will understand." Mariah's tone was soothing and kind.

"You will just have to follow my mama's example and behave as if nothing has happened," Mariah advised. "With your cool pale beauty, you have always had the enviable ability to appear unruffled. I will

be at the assembly ball with you, as will Caro and
Lord Farren."

Julia groaned aloud. "Goodness knows what Caro
told Clive. He has been polite, but I have the feeling
that he does not know what to think of me anymore.
The ramifications of that kiss seem as if they will
follow me forever." *In so many ways*, she added to
herself. "I will get through these next few days, and
then I shall go home. I *must* get away, I *must* try to
forget everything that has occurred."

Leaning back against the cushions, she turned her
gaze to the window that faced the back garden. The
early afternoon sun shone brilliantly on the stone
folly, and Julia recalled how she had stayed there in
the rain after the duke had left her. *"I may be a rakehell, but you, my dear Julia, are a hypocrite."* The harshly
spoken words still reverberated through her being.

With an attempt to push away the heartsick pain,
she turned to her friend, and with false brightness said,
"What are you going to wear to the Upper Rooms?"

Upon returning to the townhouse after a bruising
ride in the open country beyond the limits of Bath,
Kel was met in the foyer by his grandmother's
stoic butler.

"Their Graces desire your presence in the drawing
room, Your Grace." The hesitation in the old servant's
voice was no doubt due to Kel's black expression.

Brows raised in surprise, he handed the man his
hat, gloves, and crop before striding to the room
where his relatives were waiting. They were seated
facing the doorway in obvious anticipation of his
arrival.

After making a passable leg, he moved to the fireplace where he leaned a forearm on the marble
mantel.

"It must be something serious if the two of you

are sitting here in perfect harmony waiting for me. And where is my sister? I am surprised that she is not here as reinforcement," he stated, his deep voice laced with amusement.

"Emmaline, for some reason, wanted no part of this and has gone shopping. Millicent and I are in accord because of our concern for you," his grandmother stated firmly. "Please be seated, Wenlock."

His mother gestured to the chair near the fireless grate. "Yes, my dear, sit. You know we have never interfered in your affairs before, yet . . ." His mother's voice faded to a nervous little laugh.

"Yet, this time, something quite serious has come to our attention," his grandmother completed for her daughter-in-law as she stared at her grandson closely.

Moving to the chair, he met his grandmother's gaze. "Indeed? Please assuage my curiosity. You have my complete attention." He struggled to keep his tone polite, while cursing himself anew for not leaving this blasted town after the Farrens' party.

He lowered his tall frame into the chair and waited. The ladies were silent for a moment. His grandmother looked grim and his mother plucked fretfully at the fringe of her shawl. Then, by some unspoken agreement, his grandmother took the lead.

"Under normal circumstances I pay no heed to idle gossip. But when it is repeated by several trustworthy persons and is so closely connected with a member of my family . . . well, I cannot remain silent."

Kel stifled a weary sigh at his grandmother's dramatics. "I am waiting patiently to hear this dreadful gossip."

"It has come to my attention that Miss Allard, whom I admit thoroughly took me in with her pleasing ways and good humor, is quite beyond the pale."

Kel's posture immediately stiffened, and his gaze narrowed slightly. "Go on."

"I have heard that your own good friend, Lord Haverstone, claims that he has witnessed Miss Allard kissing men on a public street in London! A delightful woman I recently met at the Pump Room confirmed this information. Mrs. Marsh is from Chippenham and confided in me that Miss Allard, though from a fine and respectable family, has been the subject of speculation in her village for more than a year. Evidently, she was sent home from London because of her shocking behavior."

"Good God," Kel gritted out. "What else have you heard?"

The older woman gestured for his mother to continue. Gazing at her son with concerned brown eyes, she shifted uncomfortably in her chair before speaking.

"Well, I was told that Miss Allard was sent to Bath to escape a scandal because she behaved badly in London. I was also told that she was the subject of some sort of wager. I know you have spent some time with Miss Allard, so we thought it best that you should be informed," she said, sending her son a gentle smile.

"No one told you of whom she was accused of kissing on the street in London?" Kel asked sharply, his gaze moving from one lady to the other.

"No, but that hardly matters," his grandmother said with a shrug.

"It does." His tone was harsh as he rose from the chair. "What the gossips who were so eager to spread misinformation did not inform you was that I am the man she is accused of kissing."

The ladies jaws dropped in unison.

"What rubbish," his grandmother stated roundly.

He sent his grandmother a grim smile. "Actually,

it is not rubbish. Amazing that the tattle mongers left that bit out."

"Bless me!" His mother finally managed to gasp. "You cannot expect people to tell me to my face that my son is part of this sordid tale."

He strode to the door. Once there, he turned back to his relatives. "It is not sordid. At least not on Miss Allard's part. Please understand this completely, Miss Allard did not kiss anyone. I kissed her."

His grandmother opened and closed her mouth like a caught fish, before asking, "Whatever for?"

"Because I am a selfish libertine, and she was the loveliest creature I had ever beheld. Now I shall be going out. I may be some time, but I request that you not leave this house until I return. When I do, I will have much to discuss with both of you."

A short while later, as he rode his chestnut gelding through the quaint streets of Bath, the events of the last few weeks became clear to Kel.

He now understood Julia's oddly changeable behavior. When he had first apologized to her at Sydney Gardens, then met her again by chance at Lady Farren's tea, he had found her coolness toward him understandable—even admirable, for her behavior had been free of the vaporish drama that many women of his acquaintance would have displayed.

She was obviously self-possessed and intelligent. Also, there was a certain lack of vanity, yet acceptance of her beauty, that he found honest and appealing.

Then came Lady Farren's ball. The only reason he had agreed to escort Emmaline was that she had accused him of pacing around like a panther. He had been bored, and an evening out would occupy some time.

When he had watched Miss Allard crossing the room, he had fully expected her to again direct those beautiful, cool gray eyes right through him as she had done before. Instead, the sudden, unexpected warmth of her gaze had surprised him—and stirred his blood as well as his curiosity.

It did not take him long to suspect that something was brewing beneath the surface of her sphinxlike beauty.

In the middle of the rainstorm, when she had all but admitted that she had been blatantly teasing him in an attempt to exact revenge, he had dismissed part of her anger as embarrassment over Haverstone's thoughtless and shocking pronouncement.

Now, after the information his mother and grandmother had just imparted, he had a clearer understanding of Julia's actions.

Arriving at Haverstone's rented townhouse, he ignored the butler and strode straight to the library.

He found Haverstone, Alton, Morton, and Mattonly lounging around the dark-paneled room, with loosened neckcloths and half-empty glasses.

"It's Kel," Haverstone drawled with pleasure. " 'Bout time you came around, Your Grace. Dreadfully early to be imbibing, but it's the only thing that has held our interest since descending upon this deadly dull place. Pour yourself a whiskey and join us."

Kel stood in the middle of the room as the others lifted their glasses to him in an indolent greeting.

"No, thank you, Haverstone. I am here on an important matter."

At this statement, Lord Alton pushed his pudgy frame into a sitting position on the window seat. "I say, Kel, the last time I saw you look like this, someone got hurt."

Kel did not respond and turned his gaze to each of his friends before he spoke. "Well, my fine-feathered idiots, you have done a grand job of helping me make a muck of things. Although it is undoubtedly too late, I intend to try to repair the matter. I expect all of you to help me."

Silence held the men for a moment as they stared at Kel in surprise.

"Well then, men," Haverstone began, his drawl vanished. "Put down your glasses and let's bend an ear to our friend."

Chapter Twenty-two

"*I* am immensely proud to be in the company of the two loveliest ladies in all of Bath," Uncle John said as he escorted his wife and niece into the ballroom.

Julia did her best to smile at her uncle's compliment as she scanned the assemblage for Mariah.

"My, I forgot how lovely this room is," Aunt Beryl said, obviously excited about the prospect of a ball.

Since her aunt and uncle's arrival yesterday, there had been little time for serious conversation. For that, Julia was deeply grateful. Only once did her aunt and uncle show concern over Julia. During dinner last night, Aunt Beryl had gazed at Julia curiously. "You are awfully quiet, my dear. Is all well?"

"Of course," Julia had said with forced cheerfulness over her glass of wine. "I suspect I am a bit fatigued from the round of entertainments I have been attending. I am so glad you are here. I have missed you both very much."

Her relatives had smiled in response, and the conversation had continued without any more references to Julia's unusually quiet demeanor.

Now, in the midst of the crowded, noisy ballroom, Julia prayed that nothing would occur to renew their questions.

Espying Caro and Clive nearby, Julia felt a hint of relief. If her friends and family surrounded her, the prospect of getting through the evening was not so daunting.

"There you are," Caro called as she and Clive approached. "Now, Aunt Beryl, Uncle John, you must join every dance so that you may get your fill, for you will not have any entertainment so fine in Chippenham."

"We intend to, niece," Uncle John said jovially, looking quite elegant in his formal black evening wear.

Due to Aunt Beryl's last-minute decision to change from a lovely, raw silk, russet gown to a creamy yellow gown with a matching feathered toque, they were late and the music had already begun.

The little group stood together watching the other guests perform the graceful, measured movements of a quadrille. Julia forced herself to breathe normally. Standing at her uncle's side, she fiddled with her fan and surreptitiously glanced around the room.

Alarm bells went off in her mind as she saw several clusters of people looking in her direction and obviously whispering behind their fans and programs.

Caro must have noticed, too, for she sent Julia a quick, concerned glance. Casting a swift look to her aunt and uncle, Julia was relieved to see nothing but enjoyment in their expressions.

But to her dismay, she saw Clive's expression grow more grim at every passing measure of music. Since the night of the party, it had been apparent that his opinion of her had changed greatly.

The arrival of Mariah and Mrs. Thorncroft was a welcome diversion. As the greetings went around, Julia exchanged a speaking look with her friend. The concern beneath Mariah's smile was obvious to Julia. She gave an inward groan and prayed again that this evening would pass quickly. In just a few days, she would be able to return home with her aunt and uncle to nurse her bruised heart.

Why her heart should be bruised was a matter she forced herself not to examine.

Aunt Beryl and Uncle John joined the next dance, a minuet. Clive kindly asked Mrs. Thorncroft for the honor, leaving the three friends in relative privacy.

"Not to worry, Julia. There are a few whispers going around the room, but I doubt there will be a repeat of what happened at my party," Caro said as soon as the others were out of hearing range.

"I just hope my aunt and uncle will not notice anything amiss."

"They are enjoying themselves too much to be aware of a few gawks and whispers."

"Let us hope my mama-in-law does not locate us in this crowd. She is likely to say anything."

"Heavens! I forgot about your mama-in-law." Now Julia was truly worried.

Twenty minutes later, a flushed and happy-looking Aunt Beryl and Uncle John rejoined their nieces. Pleasant talk ensued of how talented the orchestra was and how skillful the dancers were. Julia was more than content to allow the conversation to flow over her.

From across the room, she saw Mr. Dillingham weaving his way through the crowd in her direction. She lifted her chin slightly and stiffened her spine. The look on his face after Lord Haverstone had made his shocking pronouncement was still fresh in her mind.

"Here is Mr. Dillingham! Now, there is a graceful dancer," Caro said without thinking.

Aunt Beryl and Uncle John turned to see whom Caro was referring to, when the gentleman sent one cold glance to Julia and walked past without so much as a nod.

"What a dreadful man! Never say you have an acquaintance with such a boorish creature," Aunt Beryl said, gazing after Mr. Dillingham in surprise at the obvious slight.

Uncle John frowned. "I hope that is not an example of Bath manners."

"Er . . . no, indeed. I cannot imagine why he behaved so," Caro offered.

By then, the very perceptive Aunt Beryl began to notice that Julia was upset. "My dear? Is something amiss?"

"No, Aunt. Do you think it is rather warm in here?" she said breathlessly, hoping to change the subject.

To her surprise and dread, she saw the duke's sister, Lady Fallbrook approaching. Everyone turned in surprise when the lady said, "Good evening, Miss Allard. I was hoping to have the pleasure of your company tonight. How do you do, Lord and Lady Farren?"

Thankfully, instinct took over, and Julia was able to introduce the rest of her companions. She knew that her aunt and uncle could not help but admire the lovely lady, who was exquisitely garbed in a deep green gown with emeralds and diamonds at her ears and neck. Lady Fallbrook appeared in no hurry to leave, and to Julia's further surprise, her mother, the Duchess of Kelbourne, joined them a moment later. The duchess seemed just as pleased to stay.

Julia caught Aunt Beryl's glance. The expression on her face showed how impressed she was with Julia's grand friends.

Again, Julia made the introductions, and a pleasant conversation ensued. After Lady Fallbrook and the duchess finally left the little group, Aunt Beryl turned to Julia excitedly. "What delightful acquaintances you have made! Such grace! Such ease of manners!"

Julia was enormously relieved that neither her aunt nor her uncle seemed to make the connection between the duchess and the man who had accosted her last year. It was astounding to Julia that those two illustrious ladies would deign to seek her out so pointedly, especially now.

However, there were more surprises for Julia. Moments later, the duke's grandmother sailed toward her from across the room.

Looking every inch the duchess, the dowager gazed imperiously at Julia and the others as they all curtsied or bowed before her.

"Miss Allard, you may present your friends to me."

With a slightly shaking voice, Julia did so. For once, even her unflappable aunt and uncle looked nonplussed.

Completely ignoring everyone but Julia, the dowager said, "I hope you have noticed that my daughter-in-law and granddaughter have paid you a great compliment."

"Why, yes, Your Grace." Julia gazed at the older lady in complete confusion.

"And as you can see," she continued, "I have walked across the room to speak with you. This is something I have not done for anyone since before I was married."

"I am very aware of the honor you are bestowing . . ."

"Yes, yes, yes." The dowager impatiently waved away Julia's words. "I shall continue to converse with you for a few minutes longer. I certainly hope you will know how to behave in the next half hour, Miss Allard."

Exchanging shocked glances with Mariah and

Caro, Julia could only wonder if the dowager duchess was a touch off her head.

As good as her word, the dowager stood with them, making idle small talk about the weather before taking her leave some minutes later.

"Good gracious! What next?" Caro asked everyone in general.

"Something odd is afoot," Aunt Beryl said in a mystified tone.

Suddenly, the familiar strain of a popular melody filled the room. The crowd began to murmur in surprise and confusion.

"That is not a waltz, is it?" Caro asked on a gasp.

"I do believe it is," Mariah responded, just as surprised.

"But the Master of Ceremonies does not allow waltzes," Mrs. Thorncroft stated, frowning up at the orchestral alcove.

The wide expanse of floor was empty of dancers. The murmurs grew louder as the confusion spread. Mrs. Thorncroft was correct, Julia thought, gazing around in confusion. The waltz was still considered quite scandalous and was never played at an assembly ball in stuffy Bath. What on earth was happening, she wondered.

An audible gasp rose in the room, and Julia turned her gaze to see the dowager Duchess of Kelbourne take the floor with the Earl of Haverstone. Despite the vast difference in their ages, they instantly began to move in graceful accord counterclockwise around the parquet.

A moment later Lady Fallbrook and Lord Mattonly joined the dowager and Lord Haverstone. Next came the Duke of Kelbourne's mother and the less adroit Lord Alton.

Julia felt her jaw slacken in surprise. Of the hundreds of people filling the ballroom, exactly three couples were dancing. The fact that the dancers were the highest-ranking personages in the room only added to the general surprise and speculation.

At the edge of the floor, Julia caught sight of the Master of Ceremonies, Mr. King, looking quite red in the face and mopping his brow with his handkerchief. Next to him, looking grim but calm, was the Duke of Kelbourne.

A feeling of near faintness assailed Julia, and she gripped Mariah's arm for support.

"I see him," Mariah whispered. "I suspected he was behind this."

"But why?" Julia whispered back, her heart suddenly thumping into a heady gallop.

To her utter shock, the duke began to stroll across the floor toward her. His intense gaze found hers, holding it until he was upon her.

In a tone of voice several dozen people could easily hear, he said, "Miss Allard, would you do me the honor of joining me in this dance?"

Something in the way he gazed at her caused a frisson of heightened awareness to travel up her spine. What could he be about, she wondered, gazing up at him in mystification.

The thought to decline his request swirled in her confused mind. Surely, only more pain could come from this.

You, my dear Julia, are a hypocrite. His words came to her again. Suddenly, she could no longer deny the truth of them.

Unheeding of her aunt and uncle, or anyone else, she dipped into a brief, graceful curtsy.

"Thank you, Your Grace," she said in a tone of quiet simplicity.

The look of surprise that briefly flashed across his features caused her to wonder even more at his actions.

He held out his hand, and she placed hers in his firm grasp as he led her to the floor.

For a brief, panic-stricken instant, Julia could not recall how to waltz. She need not have worried, for as soon as his hand went to her waist, she was easily able to follow his lead.

As he guided her through the first turn, he said, "I must admit that I am astounded that you agreed to waltz with me."

Lifting her eyes from the snowy folds of his beautifully tied neckcloth, she met his piercing gaze. "Then why did you ask me?"

"My desire was to afford you the satisfaction of giving me the cut direct in front of everyone. I thought the best way to call attention to the slight was by arranging a waltz."

Julia could only stare up at him in stunned silence at this pronouncement.

"Having said this," he continued, "I am grateful that you have given me this opportunity to offer you my deepest—and most regrettably late—apologies for all that I have caused you to suffer this past year."

At the simple sincerity in his voice, Julia felt heavy tears clog her throat.

They continued to swing in graceful rhythm for a few measures as the avidly curious guests looked on.

"I can only say, by way of explanation, not excuse, that I left London almost immediately after our encounter and had no notion that my friends had been looking for you. I also did not know that the people in your village would have seen your unexpected return from London as something suspect. I confess that I never gave it any consideration. I no longer wonder that you dismissed my apology out of hand—it was insufficient to the level of insult I handed you. Although I apologized, my selfish want

was to assuage my feeling of guilt for accosting you.
I now completely understand your . . . unique way
of repaying me."

The grimness of his tone galvanized a desire in
Julia to say something to lighten the dark expression
on his handsome features.

"Since I could not challenge you to pistols at dawn,
I came up with the only means at my disposal," she
managed to say.

His face was still grim despite the strained smile
that came to his lips.

"The weapon of feminine wiles is sharper than any
sword—I have learned a lesson I shall never forget.
I owe you a deeper apology for accusing you of hy-
pocrisy. You were very correct in your assessment of
my arrogance. Who am I to judge your behavior
when my own has been unpardonable?"

Silence held them again as Julia digested his words
while they continued to dance in perfect, graceful
harmony.

"But I have been a hypocrite," she finally said,
lifting her gaze to his.

The sudden, inexplicable change that came over
his face caused her heart to skip a beat.

The music faded to silence. They came to a halt,
and the duke drew her hand through his arm. As he
escorted her back to her family, he looked down at
her and said, "Miss Allard, I . . ."

"Julia, I believe it would be best if we returned to
the townhouse." Her uncle's firm voice cut through
the duke's softly spoken words. "I believe we have
much to discuss."

Before the duke had completed his bow, Julia was
being led from the ballroom, flanked by her uncle
and aunt.

Chapter Twenty-three

"*B*ut you do not understand," Julia stated, facing her uncle with defiance for the first time in her life.

He continued to pace, while she stood in the middle the room. Aunt Beryl looked on from the sofa with concern.

"Then explain to me what it is that I do not comprehend," Uncle John said in a tone of great patience.

Julia sighed heavily and looked to the heavens for the words she was struggling to find. More than anything, she wished she could have followed Caro and Clive up the stairs when they had announced upon their return from the Upper Rooms that they were retiring. Julia did not blame them for not wanting to be a part of her confrontation with their aunt and uncle.

Nevertheless, she knew that she must try to make them understand her behavior at the Upper Rooms, though she scarce understood it herself. "It is so very hard to explain. But the Duke of Kelbourne is not the horrible man we thought him to be."

"Is he, or is he not the scoundrel who kissed you in front of the world last year in London?"

"He is. But if you could have heard the sincerity of his apology . . ."

"He has once again caused you to be the object of scandalous speculation! Your aunt and I have heard of how thoroughly you loathe this man. Yet, you waltz with him in open defiance of the rules of the assembly rooms! Explain that." His pale gray eyes, so like her own, gazed at her in confusion and concern.

"The duke had no expectation that I would agree to dance with him. He was giving me the opportunity to snub him in front of everyone—as a way of showing how deeply sorry he is for what he did last year."

Throwing up his hands, her uncle cast a harried look to his wife. "This is beyond strange, Julia. I no longer know what to say to you."

Julia did not know what to say either.

"My dear," Aunt Beryl began gently, "do you care for the duke?"

Turning her troubled gaze to her aunt, Julia felt the truth rise up with her.

"Yes. *Yes.*" As she said the words, she suddenly and fully understood them to be true.

"Good God," Uncle John expostulated. "How can you care for an unmitigated, degenerate rakehell?"

"Hush for a moment, John," Aunt Beryl said calmly. "Julia, I have a suspicion that much has transpired since you came to Bath. You have left a lot out of your letters."

Tears trembled in her voice as Julia found the words to respond to her aunt. "Yes, so much has happened, I do not know where to begin. The duke is truly not what we thought. If you could see the way he treats his mother, grandmother, and sister—and how they treat him in return—you would know that he is of good character. If you could have seen the kindness he has shown Mariah and Mrs. Thorncroft, you would know that he is not truly bad."

Uncle John stopped pacing, and Aunt Beryl rose from the sofa.

"And do you believe the duke cares for you?"

Julia looked at Aunt Beryl with wide, sad eyes. She could not tell her aunt that she had caused the duke to desire her and that she had learned that, for gentlemen, desire was not love.

"Not the way I care for him," Julia replied quietly. "I know it is passing strange that I have grown to love him after what occurred, but how can these things be explained? You have told me yourself, Aunt Beryl, that the ways of the heart are truly mysterious."

A heavy knock on the front door halted her next words.

"Who could that be at this hour?" Aunt Beryl looked at her husband with a frown. "John, please tell the footman that we are not at home."

Uncle John left the room, and Julia gazed at the deep concern etched on her aunt's beloved features.

Her disgruntled uncle reentered the room, saying, "I told the footman not to answer. Whoever it is can return at a decent hour tomorrow."

Sighing with deep sadness, Julia wanted this painful interview to end.

Before her uncle could begin questioning her again, she said, "It really does not matter what my feelings toward the duke are. I shall be returning home with you and must do my best to forget him."

An unexpected, overwhelming thought suddenly gripped Julia. What if . . .

"Forgive me—I must go and see . . ." Quick as a flash, she raced across the room, to the foyer and out the front door to the front steps. Breathing heavily in the sudden, cool darkness, she looked for whoever had knocked.

A little ways down the lane, by the meager lamp-post light, she could see his familiar tall outline walking away.

Silently, she ran down the steps, across the walkway to the lane. He must have heard her, for he halted his progress and turned around.

Standing poised to run, Julia felt as if her heart were in her throat. Desperately, she struggled for words.

The duke took a few steps toward her and began to speak in a voice she hardly recognized.

"My apologies for calling so late. I walked here because I could not wait for my horse to be brought around. I wanted to ask why . . . You told me you had been a hypocrite—Julia, I must know . . ."

At the ragged passion in his voice, she closed her eyes and felt a thrill of joy sing through her heart. In an instant she was running to him. He met her more than halfway.

She stopped within a yard of him, trying desperately to see his features. To see if his expression matched the passion in his voice.

"I have been a hypocrite," she began, tossing away any lingering fear of rejection. "I thought I hated you, but soon that feeling left and I did not know what to think anymore."

He took a step nearer. "In the alcove—when you were in my arms, you had forgotten about revenge for a moment. What passed between us at that moment had been real."

"Yes," her voice was strong despite the slight tremulous tone.

"And when I kissed you in the storm . . ."

"I was not acting then, I just could not tell you that I no longer desired to hurt you."

"I suspected you were hiding your true emotions from me. I do not blame you, I have given you little reason to trust me."

Feeling a well of unexpected emotion rise within her, Julia struggled to speak. "I trust you now, Kel."

In the next instant she felt herself lifted off the ground. Throwing her arms around his neck, she could barely see his face, but she felt the fierce pounding of his heart against hers.

"Julia," he whispered roughly, as his lips met hers. Tightening her arms around him, she pressed herself against him and kissed him back with all of the intensity of her newfound love and passion.

Dragging his lips from hers, he pressed kisses to her cheek. "You are the most amazing, unexpected, beautiful, intelligent—I adore you. I have thought of little else but you since that day in London. I have loved you from the moment I saw you again in Sydney Gardens, when your beautiful gray eyes shot daggers at me. Say you will continue to lead me on a merry chase for the rest of our lives." His lips returned to hers, kissing her with a passion that made her feel as if she were melting into his body.

She tried to answer him without speaking.

In the sitting room, Aunt Beryl and Uncle John stood looking out of the window.

"I am going out there at once! They are embracing openly on a public street!" Letting the drapery fall back, Uncle John made a move to the door.

Aunt Beryl placed a restraining hand on her husband's arm and gazed lovingly into his concerned eyes. "Come and sit with me, my love. Evidently embracing our niece in public is a habit the Duke of Kelbourne is not likely to break."

Epilogue

1817

On a fine spring day, the Duke and Duchess of Kelbourne were taking a leisurely stroll down a very fashionable street in London.

Suddenly, the duchess stopped and looked up at her husband in delighted surprise.

"Kel, this is it!" She gestured to the storefront they had just passed. "This is the shop I stepped out of that day."

"I believe it is," said Kel. Reaching down, he took her gloved hand and raised it to his lips.

"Gracious, that day seems a hundred years ago. So much has happened since. What was the wager? Dame Fortune? A boxing match? I no longer recall," she said with a tease.

Turning her hand palm up, he pushed aside the top of her glove. Then he placed a warm, lingering kiss on her wrist, before gazing passionately into her eyes. "My darling Julia, do you not know by now that the only thing wagered that day was my heart?"